Dynamo

Mech Wars Book 2

Scott Bartlett

Mirth Publishing
St. John's

DYNAMO

© Scott Bartlett 2017

Cover art by: Tom Edwards (tomedwardsdesign.com)

Library and Archives Canada Cataloguing in Publication

Bartlett, Scott

Dynamo / Scott Bartlett ; illustrations by Tom Edwards.

ISBN 978-1-988380-08-7

To my mother, Valerie.

CHAPTER 1

Into the Shadows

As Gabe and Jake Price sprinted toward the tunnel mouth, the earth was still vomiting up Quatro by the dozens.

Oneiri Team was fighting hard, but it wasn't enough. The aliens were still managing to get between them to attack what remained of Darkstream's reserve battalion, the Force Multipliers, along with the soldiers from Plenitos' garrison.

Bayonets extended from several of the Quatro's backs, and they gouged at the humans viciously while the other aliens mostly hung back to pelt the soldiers with artillery, which was also strapped to their backs.

How the aliens managed to operate the firearms remained a mystery—but it wasn't the most mysterious thing about them.

"Hit them with everything we have," Gabe growled over the team-wide. "Do not let them reach the hills. If that happens, this is all over."

And so the MIMAS mech pilots stepped up their game. For his part, Gabe extended both bayonets as he slammed into the first wave of Quatro, skewering two of them at once, and withdrawing the blades to plunge them into alien flesh again.

His targets down, Gabe engaged both flamethrowers, criss-crossing the long streams of flame as he took one hard-fought step after another.

The fire flickered over the shapes of allies and enemies alike, casting them in sharp relief. It wasn't just that: everything had a hyper-realness to it, which Gabe took as the dream rendering the urgency of keeping the Quatro away from what he and Price had discovered in the hills behind them.

It was hard to fathom the timing. Just as they'd emerged from the tunnel, after being pursued by a pair of Quatro with the unexpected power to stop bullets in midair, Price had spotted unusually colored meteorites streaking toward the planet.

He and Gabe had investigated, and what they'd found troubled Gabe as much as it confused him: mechs, clearly of alien make, and just as clearly built for Quatro to use.

Having cleared the area in front of him, Gabe instructed his mech's hands to retract, splitting to settle back against his wrists as he spun up the rotary autocannons they revealed.

Armor-piercing shells sped through the air—more than enough to part Quatro flesh and rupture their innards. Providing they didn't stop the rounds before they struck their target, using the same magic trick they'd used underground.

They didn't. The Quatro no longer seemed to have the ability to halt bullets in midair, for reasons just as inscrutable as the power's existence before.

Was I hallucinating?

No. His mental state had been iffy, lately—even he could see that—but the others had also seen what the Quatro had done.

Besides, if he'd hallucinated that, then he'd also hallucinated Tommy's death.

I know when I've lost a soldier. I wouldn't just dream up something like that.

Gabe added Tommy's death to the long list of things for which he intended to repay the Quatro. Never mind that it had happened while the Darkstream soldiers were invading the aliens' home. They'd deserved that, too. They deserved everything that had happened to them, as well as everything Gabe intended to do to them.

Having driven the Quatro front back, Gabe reformed his hands in front of the autocannons, switching to rockets. The other members of Oneiri had followed a progression of weapons similar to Gabe's, and together they'd had the desired effect, of pushing the Quatro farther and farther back toward the tunnel mouth.

At last, the aliens began to slip into the shadows, disappearing from the surface of Eresos.

Slithering back into their dank holes. Where they belong.

Gabe switched to a battalion-wide channel, so that everyone could hear his orders. Bronson had given him the command, which was lucky. He doubted any of Arkady Black's people would appreciate the gravity of the situation they faced, and the same went for the remnants of the late Benjamin Clifford's Force Multipliers.

To prevent humanity from getting wiped from the face of Eresos—maybe even the whole system—he was glad to have the command.

"I want both the soldiers of Plenitos' garrison and the Force Multipliers to continue guarding the tunnel mouth. Oneiri Team, to me."

As he spoke the last words, Gabe jogged to the edge of his forces, allowing enough space for the giant MIMAS mechs to gather around him.

They did, many of them stowing artillery as they ran, metal parts clicking together with a pleasing cleanness.

All of Oneiri's mechs appeared to have retained one hundred percent functionality, even after several battles, which spoke highly of Darkstream's engineering. That said, they'd suffered a fair amount of superficial damage. Price's MIMAS looked singed from the bottom-up, with his feet almost totally black while above his elbows was barely touched. Ash Sweeney's torso was crumpled slightly near the center, though the damage wasn't serious.

Almost all of the mechs were scored in several places, whether by the Quatro's bayonets, their claws, or their knife-like fangs.

"I'll keep this short, since I don't know how much time we have," Gabe said over the team-wide. "When Price and I went into the hills to investigate the meteorites, we found mechs that appear to have been designed for Quatro use. Someone's screwing with humanity, and judging by these quadruped mechs' similarity to the Gatherers and Amblers, the culprit seems likely to be whoever made those."

He let that sink in. Other than a couple of glances exchanged between some of the team members, everyone remained silent.

Gabe had told them of the need for haste, and he was glad to see they didn't impede that with any stupid questions.

"Our task right now is to locate as many of these Quatro mechs as we can find. If we miss even one, it could mean disaster for every human settlement on Eresos. I hope I don't need to explain why."

He looked around expectantly at his team. No one seemed to require an explanation.

If Tommy was still alive, he'd probably need one.

The thought was callous, but he was prone to those, especially lately.

"Good," he said. "Move out."

The MIMAS mechs spread through the hills.

CHAPTER 2

Quads

"Found another quad, sir," Beth Arkanian said. "You wanna check this one out, too?" They'd settled on the name "quads" for the quadruped mechs naturally enough.

It fits well enough, I suppose.

Gabe considered Beth's question. This was the eighth quad they'd found. "Does it look similar to the others?"

"Yes, sir."

"Then I'm good. Send the Force Multipliers its coordinates, and tell them I said to back up a personnel carrier next to it. Gonzalez, Sweeney, and Price, help Arkanian to load the quad aboard."

They'd discovered that if they stripped out one of the Force Multipliers' armored personnel carriers, they could just fit two of the quads inside.

"Why don't we just destroy them, sir?" Price had asked when Gabe first gave the order to load the quads onto the personnel carriers.

Gabe had turned toward him. "Remember when I said, back on Plenitos' walls, that I welcome decent suggestions from my subordinates?"

"Yes, sir."

"This isn't one of them. If the quads are anything like the alien mech your father found out in the Belt, their armor's as strong as hell. I'm not sure we even have enough ammunition to destroy them, and if we ran out before we finished the job, the quads would become easy pickings for the Quatro. Better to save our ammo for the aliens themselves."

"Makes sense. Thanks for breaking that down for me, sir."

Gabe couldn't hear any sarcasm in Price's voice, but the boy had given him attitude before, and he was always on the lookout for it. Even if he hadn't been at his wits' end, he wouldn't have wanted to continue putting up with it, and he certainly didn't plan to while he was this on edge.

"What about Tommy's mech, sir?" Marco Gonzalez asked after they'd finished loading the latest quad.

Glancing toward the tunnel mouth, Gabe grimaced, which manifested inside the dream as the sky flashing emerald three times in rapid succession.

Tommy's abandoned mech stood alone, arms extended forward slightly, looking as though it was ready to do battle.

But it won't. At least, it wouldn't until Oneiri Team gained another qualified mech pilot. Backup pilots had been trained, but they were still up on Valhalla Station as far as he knew, and Tommy's mech was all the way out here.

"We're going to have to secure it to one of the tanks. It'll impair the tank's functionality, but it's all we can do. We can't leave a MIMAS out here for a mercenary to stumble across."

For two more hours, they combed the hills near the entrance to the Quatro tunnels. But after the eighth quad that Beth had found, no more turned up.

Which was lucky, considering they'd run out of personnel carriers to transport them in. Gabe didn't want to impair another tank if he could avoid it.

"All right, then," he said over the battalion-wide. "We have a journey ahead of us. I want these quads off this planet, as fast as we can make that happen. Which means we're headed back to Ingress. We don't have shuttles big enough to ferry them up to Valhalla, and I'm sure as hell not crawling inside one of those things to check whether they have launch capability. So the space elevator's our only option. Let's roll out."

Without further ceremony, they started down the same Gatherer path they'd taken to get here.

Gabe had wanted Oneiri Team to take a long break in Plenitos—to rest, but also to spend time out of their mechs.

Inside the MIMAS mechs, each member of Oneiri Team felt powerful, nigh-indestructible. Outside of them, they felt small, vulnerable...weak.

They were becoming increasingly dependent on the machines, not only physically, but psychologically. Gabe had already noticed a few of his Oneiri soldiers walking with slumped shoulders outside their mechs, and he'd snapped at them to straighten up. They no longer walked with confidence, with heads high. No, they reserved that for their mechs, now.

None of them brought up any of that, of course. But Gabe could see it in them. And he recognized it in himself.

That wasn't all. Gabe had also come to find that piloting the mechs had a disquieting *distancing* effect. The dream, which had been meant to increase immersion in battle, was instead causing him to feel detached from its effects, its consequences.

The dream made him feel justified in everything he did, by default. That was more or less how he'd always felt anyway, but now he didn't even bother to examine his own actions, and that was starting to get to him. Especially during the fleeting moments he spent outside of the mech, which seemed to be characterized by a lot more self-reflection than when he was inside the thing.

And so, he'd wanted his team to take time in their own bodies, to reconnect with their humanity.

But the quads' arrival had dashed that hope. Now, they'd have to spend weeks more in the mechs, weeks full of long days of journeying. No one else could pilot the mechs for them—no one else was authorized to, for good reason.

Until the quads were safely aboard the space elevator and on their way to Valhalla, Oneiri Team would live inside their mechs.

CHAPTER 3

Classic Conspiracy Theorist

As she walked, Lisa sighted down the barrel of her assault rifle at the ground.

I need to calibrate the sight again.

She'd had to do that several times since leaving Alex's wilderness for the confines of Habitat 2. The planet had given her a souvenir in the form of its blue dust, which had filled every crevice of her body, clothes, and weaponry. She'd dealt with the first two with multiple washings, but her guns were posing a stiffer challenge. She'd probably have to dismantle and clean them yet again.

Tessa had joined Lisa on her rounds, patrolling the streets of Habitat 2. With drug crime either eliminated or driven deep underground in the wake of Daybreak's defeat, she didn't expect to encounter much that needed her attention, but that wasn't really what this was about.

After what they'd been subjected to, living under the thumb of Quentin Cooper and his goons for two months, the people of

Habitat 2 needed to see that Darkstream military personnel were patrolling the city keeping them safe.

Unfortunately, right now, all they had in the way of Darkstream military personnel were Lisa and Tessa, and Tessa didn't even work for the company anymore. In fact, she loathed it.

"Have you given any more thought to what Samuel Dalton said?" Tessa said. "About Darkstream allowing Daybreak to take over Habitat 2?"

Lisa frowned. She hadn't meant for Tessa to find out about that. The guards that had brought Dalton before her had been sworn to secrecy, but they'd blabbed about the interview to Andy Miller anyway, because they knew Andy was a friend of hers and they figured it wouldn't matter.

Andy, God love him, had told Tessa.

"I'm afraid I don't consider the words of a criminal enough to indict my employer, Tessa." Lisa checked down an alley as she spoke. Nothing. As usual. "I'm going to need more than that to go against the organization that everyone's lives are built on, in the Steele System."

"Oh, that's classic," Tessa said. "Blind yourself to immense danger, because seeing the truth would be too inconvenient. Yes. I do love it when history repeats itself."

Lisa decided to change the subject. "Have you been talking to any of the Quatro lately?"

"A little. They're not much for chitchat. That said, they seem to like us a lot more than they like the rest of humanity."

Lisa nodded. "That's for sure." She sniffed, double-taking at a darkened window, which she felt pretty sure was the one she'd peered out from during her temporary imprisonment in a basement, the day Daybreak had taken over. "Rug keeps pushing to go to Eresos. She thinks they can convince their fellow Quatro to stop attacking settlements."

Tessa barked laughter, at that. "Rug doesn't even know why they're fighting. Besides, the way Rug treats most everyone in Habitat 2, I would have thought she'd *want* the Eresos Quatro to kill as many humans as possible."

Lisa turned from her study of a shadowy doorway to look at Tessa. "That isn't fair."

"I know. It was a joke. A poor one."

"All right."

"Bottom line about going to Eresos is, we have no way of doing it. I mean, we could head out toward the space elevator, I guess, but I'm not keen to get blue dust in every orifice again."

"Me neither," Lisa said. "Either way, Habitat 2 needs us. We can't leave now."

"We'll have to leave eventually, though," Tessa said. It was her turn to study Lisa's face. "If you're to keep the promise you made to the Quatro, that is."

"I intend to. I'll figure out a way to do it. Just not yet."

That seemed to satisfy the white-haired woman, and she nodded, causing her hair to sway. "Good. I'm not eager to go to Eresos, myself. Not sure I like the look of the new toys Darkstream's acquired for itself."

Lisa said nothing to that, reluctant to criticize her employer at all in front of the older woman. Although the images floating around the system net, of Darkstream mechs walking the streets of Plenitos, certainly were striking. Lisa wasn't sure she wanted to meet one, either.

I'm just glad they're with us and not against us.

A notification appeared in the upper-right of Lisa's vision, informing her she had a vid message. She played it right away—her interface's transparency settings were high enough to allow her to view media as she walked.

It was Commander Laudano, finally responding to her message asking for authorization to offer leniency to Daybreak prisoners in exchange for information on Quentin Cooper. Lisa had gone ahead and offered that leniency anyway; this message would let her know whether she could actually make good on the offer.

"Do not under any circumstances grant leniency to any of those prisoners," Laudano said.

Oops, Lisa thought.

Commander Laudano went on: "They violated the peace and prosperity of Habitat Two, and they are to be punished proportionately. Darkstream will soon send a battalion of soldiers to administer justice and also to secure Habitat 2. Laudano out."

Though she felt a little sheepish at being denied permission to do what she'd already done, she didn't feel too badly about breaking her promise to the people who'd subjugated her friends and neighbors.

Lisa forwarded the message to Tessa.

"See?" she said once the older woman had watched it. "Darkstream isn't evil, Tessa. They clearly plan to be pretty hard on these Daybreak jerks. This isn't the sort of message a company sends who wants to turn people into slaves."

"I still don't trust them," Tessa said, and fell silent.

Shaking her head, Lisa decided not to press the issue.

Tessa's a classic conspiracy theorist. She only accepts information that supports her beliefs about the company she hates.

Lisa just hoped the former soldier wouldn't cause any trouble, once the Darkstream battalion arrived.

CHAPTER 4

Valiant

Jake plodded across the hard-packed terrain, his mech towering above most of the battalion that rolled through Eresos' wilderness at a steady clip.

They'd long ago left Plenitos behind, and now they pushed through the woods that surrounded the planet's largest city for miles. Every so often, they had to stop to avoid one of the giant Amblers patrolling the Gatherer paths. The battalion had more than enough artillery to take an Ambler down, but they'd take significant, unnecessary damage in doing so.

Eventually, the woods would give way to the great Barrens that stretched between Plenitos and Ingress, where the space elevator was located.

Their forced march didn't leave much room for chatter, but even so, Jake couldn't help but notice the almost complete lack of rapport between Oneiri Team, the remnants of the Force Multipliers, and the Plenitos garrison soldiers, who'd been authorized to abandon their posts in favor of preventing the quads from falling into the hands—paws—of the Quatro.

I would have expected a little more camaraderie between brothers- and sisters-in-arms.

It didn't seem like a good sign that the three groups treated each other with vague suspicion.

I guess we all come from different places, with different short-term goals.

The garrison soldiers were used to staying in one place, digging in, and protecting the inhabitants.

This long march probably has them agitated.

Indeed, they were the ones who seemed to snap at each other the most, with voices that raised with little prompting.

The reserve battalion, the Force Multipliers, were used to going wherever the company needed them, applying extra force to meet the company's goals in a given sector.

And the MIMAS pilots were the newbies, favored by the company, and walking around in what probably seemed like newfangled contraptions to the other soldiers.

The only thing that unites us is that we're all paid to further Darkstream's position and profits.

But they had a higher aim, whether anyone acknowledged it or not. Sometimes, Jake wished they would talk about it more: by keeping the quads from the Quatro, they were sparing the people of Eresos untold suffering.

Ash drew up beside him, subvocalizing to keep their conversation private out of habit. "Hey," she said. "Have you been browsing the system net at all with your implant?"

"A little bit," he confessed. It wasn't encouraged to browse the net while operating a MIMAS, but all they were doing was walking, and he knew he could handle both.

"Did you see that they found Quatro on Alex, too? Wearing pressure suits and everything?"

"Yeah. Just full of surprises, aren't they?"

"Indeed. I can't wait to find out how they ended up there. Pretty scary, to think the ones here might have access to that level of technology. Though, you know, I'm not sure Darkstream hates the Quatro as much as they claim to."

Jake glanced at her. "Why do you say that?"

"Well, look at Ingress. The city has been trying to sell off the tunnel borer they used to dig their walls, just to cover the rising costs of their contract with Darkstream. If they ever need to do repairs on those walls, they'll be screwed."

Though he nodded, Jake didn't answer. It seemed like too much to process, just now. The constant marching was getting to him already, and he just wanted to be alone inside his own head for a bit.

Of course, the battalion couldn't walk indefinitely—they had to stop to eat, and to sleep.

If it weren't for those necessities, Chief Roach probably would never have permitted them to take the time to hold a funeral for Tommy.

"We can hold one," he said when Beth Arkanian broached the subject. "It'll mean less sleep, but we can hold one."

So they did.

If nothing else, the funeral brought them together—Oneiri Team, the Force Multipliers, and the Plenitos garrison, all gathered in a broad clearing where rays of sun broke through the forest canopy to kiss the ground.

It was also one of the few times Oneiri Team were outside their mechs, though they'd left them nearby, in case of attack.

To Jake, it felt odd not to be encased in metal and artillery, encased in the dream. It was a little exhilarating, but also a little terrifying. The track marks along his forearm caught his eye, where, whenever he needed to get out of his mech, the machine injected him with the antagonist to the sedative he used to enter lucid. That made his stomach shift uncomfortably.

Everyone bore as a mark of shame the fact that they'd been forced to abandon Tommy's mangled corpse deep within the Quatro tunnels, but given the circumstances, it didn't seem likely his body would ever be recovered.

Nothing to send back to his parents but a letter of condolence.

"Tommy never got a nickname," Beth said to those gathered. "Which is unacceptable, to be honest. He fought in the Battle of Ingress, contributing to a victory that saved that city, and he helped us retake the streets of Plenitos after the Quatro broke through her walls. But we never did him the honor of marking him as our brother by granting him a nickname. We were too caught up in the turmoil and stress of battle."

Beth cast her gaze over her fellows, over all of the Darkstream soldiers gathered in the clearing. "Tommy would probably forgive us for it. He wasn't one to hold a grudge. Even so, I still think it's unacceptable."

"I agree," Ash put in. "He's the one who gave me my nickname. Steam. Even in the heat of battle, he took the time to acknowledge my contribution, to recognize me as his sister-in-arms. Where else will we get our nicknames, if not from battle?"

"Exactly," Beth said, nodding, smiling at Ash. "That's why I'm proposing that we give Tommy a nickname now. He was a true brother. He stood by us, and he kept us all in his heart. He led the charge into the Quatro tunnels. Does anyone have an idea for a nickname that would do his memory justice?"

"Hero," Ash said.

Jake stepped forward. "Valiant."

They put it to a vote, and Valiant won out. After that, they held a ceremonial internment, with the dirt of Eresos shoveled symbolically into a shallow, empty grave.

When they departed the clearing, they left behind a sturdy cross in their wake, driven into the ground by the powerful hands of a MIMAS mech.

CHAPTER 5

Two-Legged Murderers

He stalked through the wilderness, having ranged ahead of his fellows.

A breeze rose, and he paused, lifting his nose to learn what it carried.

There. The faint stench of the enemy. Stronger than it had been the last time he'd detected it.

We're getting closer.

It was curious, how time could change your relationship with a smell. When he'd first breathed in the scent of the two-legged beasts that now infested this planet's surface, it hadn't seemed especially offensive. Now, he found it repulsive.

Back in the Home Systems—so many years ago, so many stars away—he'd been among those calling loudest for his drift to leave.

And it had worked. Now, here they were, the Grounded, reduced to a primitive, brutish life, hunted by aliens much smaller than they.

He took responsibility for that. He didn't know whether atonement was possible, but either way, he felt determined to better his drift's lot.

The memory of sailing through the stars remained vivid for him—probably because he revisited it every day. Sometimes, he wondered whether his starlust hadn't been a bigger factor in his desire to leave than the freedom his drift would gain by doing so.

Of course, it hadn't been the two-legs who'd ended their flight through the stars. No, that had been the work of the Interlopers. They'd smashed open his drift's starships, extracting them from the vessels bodily, and destroying everything that lent their lives comfort and meaning.

That done, the Interlopers had stranded them on this planet, to become the Grounded. They separated each crew by hundreds of miles, sometimes thousands. In doing so, they turned a single, unified drift into many.

Why?

He still didn't understand it. His species had never encountered the Interlopers before. The rest of his species—the majority, still back in the Home Systems, which his drift had abandoned—they had warred with the Pyleen for the better part of a decade, but the Pyleen were not known to have allies.

What had the Interlopers gained from destroying their ships and scattering them all across this world? What had they gained by turning them into the Grounded?

That had only been the start of their woes. The two-legged aliens had arrived shortly after, driving his now-splintered drift deep underground, denying them access to the resource-bearing machines that were the planet's only original occupants.

Except, he'd learned that not all the two-legs were alike. Another group of them had approached his drift very recently, shortly after an attack by the others. This new group dressed in more motley garb, and not the uniforms worn by the murderers.

The shabbily dressed two-legged drift came bearing arms, but not to use against the Grounded. Instead, they'd left them artillery—crates and crates of it—for the Grounded to use. Then, the two-legs had departed, without any attempt to communicate.

Their behavior had confused many among the Grounded, but they'd dragged their offerings underground nevertheless. As always, their powers returned to them in full force as they progressed deeper into the earth, and their superconducting brains allowed them to extract the weapons and affix them to their backs using great metal bands, which they bent and twisted to their will.

As his splintered drift armed for war, they'd sent out messengers to the other Grounded—to every other fractured drift whose location they knew. There were almost certainly many drifts of Grounded whose locations they didn't know, in caves and tunnels elsewhere on the planet. But the local ones had been enough to form a massive host, ready to visit havoc on the two-legs that had attacked them in their homes.

The Grounded's ability to manipulate metals was significantly diminished when they went aboveground, but it was enough to pull the trigger of a gun—or of a rocket launcher.

In the end, it hadn't been enough to defeat the two-legs, who'd sent mighty machines into battle; robots that towered over even the Grounded. Those had driven his drift back into their tunnels...but then the masters of the machines had made a mistake. They got out of their walking weapons, and they followed the Grounded underground.

There, they'd encountered his true might. He'd been the one to kill one of the machine masters, and after that, he'd chased the two-legs to the surface. In the battle that followed, he killed several more, though he'd had his right ear shot off in the exchange.

The two-legs had regained the advantage once they'd climbed back inside their machines. But something changed when strange objects fell from the sky...something that caused the two-legged murderers to beat a hasty retreat, instead of lingering in the area to torment the Grounded further.

I mean to find out what that something was.

Whatever it had been, it clearly frightened the two-legs. And anything that frightened them *had* to be good for his drift.

He took responsibility for what his drift had been reduced to. He felt determined to better his drift's lot.

It seemed probable that effort would start with hunting the two-legs and uncovering what had startled them so.

Having picked up the scent of the two-legged murderers once again, he turned back to notify the other Grounded that accompanied him.

CHAPTER 6

Mating Ritual Initiated

"Do you really think these humans will try anything with forty-two Quatro walking the streets?" Rug asked, the deep, rich tones of her translator filling the narrow lane.

A shopkeep sweeping her front step glanced up at the giant alien, face blank, and quickly returned to her work, keeping her head down.

Either the Quatro aren't aware of the effect they have on the residents, or they don't care.

Lisa's theory was that they *weren't* aware of it, but if they had been, they wouldn't care anyway.

"No, not really," Lisa said, speed-walking out of necessity, to keep up with the royal purple alien. "I actually think crime will probably stay as low as it has been, for a while at least. But seeing a Darkstream operative on patrol is more for their benefit than it is for security. You Quatro may keep the peace in effect, but I'm not sure you exactly instill a sense of—"

Lisa drew to an abrupt stop. "Come on, Rug. I just remembered that I left a report on my desk that needs to be filed."

But that wasn't the real reason she had for stopping, and as the Quatro peered at the street ahead, Lisa thought the alien probably sensed that. A block away from them, near the entrance to Habitat 2's only lucid arcade, Andy was standing with a girl several years younger than him. She was shoving him lightly, laughing, the sound of it grating on Lisa's ears.

Rug followed her as she turned back the way they'd come, beating a hasty retreat. The Quatro plodded along the narrow lane in silence for a time, other than her heavy footfalls, which produced a considerable amount of sound against the simulated cobble.

At last, Rug glanced backward toward Andy, which was not a discreet gesture, given the size of the alien's head. Then, she turned toward Lisa, studying her with onyx eyes.

"You seem upset by the mating ritual Andy initiated with that human female. Why?"

"I'm not upset," Lisa said, a little too tersely.

"You seem so. Which confuses me. We Quatro make all of our mating decisions based on what serves the drift. We did not reproduce at all after the Meddlers stranded us here, because of our severely limited resources. But a Quatro would have been pleased, in your place, to have witnessed Andy's act."

It was Lisa's turn to study Rug's face, though she wasn't sure why she bothered, as it was usually pretty inscrutable. "Why in Sol would they have been *pleased?*"

"Because the female with whom Andy engages in the ritual does not seem likely to attract many mates. By choosing her, Andy would serve your drift by maximizing the number of possible couplings."

Lisa laughed, then—a true laugh, which came straight from her belly to ring out in the narrow lane and bounce off the metal buildings.

"Thanks, Rug."

Somehow, the alien had managed to make her feel better. She hadn't expected that.

CHAPTER 7

Fury and Justice

A klaxon cut through the night, prompting Jake to claw his way to wakefulness. Blinking rapidly, he refused to let grogginess impede him.

Deep sleep was not a luxury afforded to soldiers.

What's going on?

The camp was a flurry of movement, with Darkstream soldiers running this way and that, snatching up guns, climbing into tanks, taking up positions behind the armored personnel carriers.

It wasn't as much information as he would have liked, but it was enough to tell him that he was almost certainly much better off *inside* his mech than outside it.

Luckily, he slept underneath the MIMAS mech, between its giant legs.

Slapping the machine's calf caused a ramp to detach from its back, popping open to lower itself to the ground. Jake clambered up it, tossing a REM sleep-inducing sedative into his mouth as he did.

Soon, he was inside the mech, the back sealing up once more as he slipped into the dream.

Then, he *was* the mech. He was its massive frame, and he was the artillery that bristled all over it.

Inside the dream, he was fury and justice and death, in metallic form.

Now to find some enemies to visit that death upon.

Charging through the camp, taking care not to knock over any of his fellows, he yelled, "What's going on?" His voice crashed like thunder.

A member of the Plenitos garrison turned toward him, white-faced, shaking. "Quatro," he said, and that was all he had time to get out.

Behind him, one of the beasts crashed through the trees, heading straight for them. The soldier hunched, raising a wavering shotgun to his face to point in the alien's general direction.

Jake stepped over the man, heedless of the shotgun, which looked like little more than a twig from inside the mech—from inside the dream.

"I'll handle this," Jake muttered as both his hands separated into segments, coming to rest against his wrists while twin rotary autocannons spun up, delivering hot death straight into the Quatro's hide. Dark spurts of blood flew into the night air, and the beast crashed into the ground well before reaching them.

There were plenty more where that came from, apparently. Before long, it seemed the Quatro were everywhere, some of them charging the human ranks, making liberal use of long bayonets, while other hung back among the trees and returned fire with the various guns strapped to their backs.

The strangled roar of a rocket leaving its tube sounded nearby, and Jake's eyes fell on the Quatro that had loosed the projectile, which headed straight toward the soldier still cowering at Jake's feet.

Jake ran forward, arms extended as though to catch the rocket. His fractured hands yet rested against his forearms, however, and he continued to fire his autocannons, armor-piercing shells peppering the oncoming missile.

The rocket exploded a meter away, and its momentum carried the explosion forward, bathing Jake's arms and head and torso in flame.

Jake *was* the mech, and what it felt, he felt. Pain lanced through his body, and he screamed with the agony of it.

He would not let it stop him, however. Striding forward despite the physical torment, he reached behind his back to detach his heavy machine gun, swinging it around to fire at the Quatro who'd launched the rocket.

The alien twisted around, desperate to evade the storm of bullets. And it succeeded for a time, the ordnance tearing up trees instead, causing them to explode into hundreds of shards of dry bark.

Then Jake caught up to it, extending both bayonets, and plunging forward with them.

The Quatro backed up, so Jake engaged both flamethrowers, directing the streams of fire in the direction where he anticipated the Quatro would go.

It worked. The creature's fur caught fire, along with the tree it crouched behind.

The alien recoiled in pain, but Jake followed, and this time his twin blades found the Quatro's flesh. The monster slumped to the ground.

Not taking any time to congratulate himself, he turned back toward the camp, which had descended into chaos during the seconds it had taken him to deal with the rocket-launching Quatro.

The invaders had infiltrated the human ranks, pushing past them, making dangerous progress toward the middle, where the personnel carriers were that housed the quadruped mechs.

Jake dashed toward them, and as he did, he noticed a particularly large Quatro briefly silhouetted against some burning trees. It looked to be missing an ear, and it was making straight for the quads, unnoticed by most of the human defenders, who were locked in furious combat with yet more aliens.

Jake *did* notice the beast, and he sprinted toward it, even as it reached the personnel carriers, disappearing behind one of them.

Seconds later, as Jake rounded the same corner, he saw what had happened: one of the personnel carriers had been blasted open, revealing the high-tech cargo inside.

The one-eared Quatro stood before the nearest quad, standing perfectly still, in stark contrast to the chaos around it.

Jake surged forward, right bayonet extended to take the beast in its haunch. But before he could, the quad opened up, its top half rising to admit the alien, who slipped inside it.

Both halves met once more, and the quad rose up, turning, its eyes aglow.

The thing's shoulders *morphed*, and giant, identical cannons took shape. The next instant, Jake was flying through the air to crash to the ground on his back, his head glancing painfully off a rock. If it had been his own head, he would have died.

By the time he got up, the quad-piloting Quatro was already halfway to the trees, bellowing wordlessly.

The other Quatro disengaged, then, turning only to conduct covering fire, to facilitate their retreat.

CHAPTER 8

Adventurous Benders

Unlike most people who'd accompanied Darkstream to the Steele System, Bob O'Toole had never actually worked for the company.

He'd been a chartered accountant back in the Milky Way, and he'd invested almost all of his discretionary income in Darkstream shares. That had paid off quite lucratively, for a long time—until the stock fell on hard times, when the company was booted clean out of the galaxy.

Ah, well. No one had ever said that playing the stock market wasn't a bit of a gamble.

Since, to continue benefiting from all that stock he owned, Bob would have to follow Darkstream to a galaxy where humans had never set foot before...well, that's exactly what he did. And although the economy the company proceeded to set up in the Steele System was much smaller than the Milky Way—yet growing rapidly!—Darkstream was paramount within it, and owning a hell of a lot of company stock was just about the best position for an expatriate accountant past his prime to find himself in.

Long story short, it meant he had a lot of credits to throw around. He could live anywhere in the Steele System he wanted. He could *do* anything he wanted. Nothing limited him. Why would it? He was rich!

And so, with all those riches, with all that limitless opportunity, he'd decided to live in Habitat 2, permanently indoors in the middle of a dusty nowhere, to become an avid alcoholic with the help of Phineas Gage, owner and sole proprietor of the Dusty Bucket.

That had been fine, for a while: hanging off the end of Gage's bar and calling out the other patrons whenever he felt like it. Then those Daybreak freaks had taken over, coked out or whatever they were, pushing everyone around and hogging most of the booze for themselves. During those dark months, Bob had paid top dollar just to buy enough grog to get a good buzz on.

But with enough credits, one could do anything. Including bribe Daybreak asshats to let him do basically whatever he wanted, like get drunk whenever he felt like it.

But those asshats had loved to come into the Dusty Bucket and stick their noses in every conversation. Plus, there hadn't been nearly as many patrons left to make fun of, what with all the slave labor that had gone on at that time.

So Bob had taken it upon himself to make friends with the nerds of Habitat 2. He used to slip them little nips of brandy or vodka or rum or whiskey or whatever he had on him at the time.

It hadn't taken much of the stuff to make the nerds love him, and once they loved him, they'd started doing little favors for him, like hacking the habitat's security feeds and giving him direct access on his implant, so he could track where the Daybreak goons were at any given time. His favorite nerd, a fellow named Wyatt, even deleted some footage for Bob, of him urinating on Quentin Cooper's hoverbike during one of his more adventurous benders.

Yes, getting friendly with the nerds was a fine thing. Almost as good as having a lot of credits, these days. And when that gorgeous brunette Lisa Sato returned with Tessa Notaras and their hairy friends to break Cooper's hold on the place, Bob had made sure to continue maintaining those friendships. Everyone loved free booze, whether they were living in a druglord's dystopia or not, so he continued to supply them with it.

It didn't take long for them to turn up something juicy for him. Something he could use, something he could take to Lisa Sato as an offering. It didn't hurt to get on the good side of a Darkstream soldier, no it didn't, and the fact that she was drop-dead stunning didn't deter him in the slightest.

"What do you want, O'Toole?" she asked, her mouth twisted into a grimace as he staggered through the door of her office.

"I brought you a present," he mumbled, scratching his backside and trying to remember whether he'd showered today.

"I'd be incredibly surprised to find myself interested in any present you would care to give me."

"Prepare to be surprised!" he said, grinning, and then he fired over the files his nerds had dug up for him.

"What are these?" Lisa said, frowning slightly as she stared into the space just over Bob's left shoulder, no doubt reviewing the files on her implant.

"Messages," Bob grunted. "Sent from our esteemed former councilman, Leonardo Fiore, to Quentin Cooper himself. Recently. Have a look. He really spills his guts, in 'em. Tells Cooper all about our security, or lack thereof. Our defenses, such as they are. And especially about the number of Quatro you brought in here. How fearsome their teeth look, and so on, and so on."

"Wow," Lisa said, inclining her head, her raven hair swaying slightly with the movement. "This is just what we need to nail Fiore to the wall."

"Well, that's not all," Bob said, scowling. "I'd love to see Fiore fingered as much as the next guy, but that isn't the most important implication of these messages. The most important thing is—"

"Cooper's planning to attack Habitat 2. Again."

"Uh, yes," Bob said. "That's exactly right."

"I'm not sure how he proposes to do that, given we killed most of his thugs, and arrested almost all of the rest. But the fact that he *thinks* he can do it is worrying on its own. Thank you for this, Bob. If there's any way I can repay you, anything I can do, say the word—just please don't say something gross."

Bob's grin fizzled. Come to think of it, he *had* been about to say something Lisa would likely find gross, coming from an old man like him.

"Ah..." He cleared his throat. "I don't need anything. Got enough drink to last me three lifetimes, I reckon. I'm good." He bobbed his head at her, turned unsteadily, and shuffled out of her office.

Wonder who wants to have a drink with me. He racked his brain, but no one came to mind.

Probably, a sip of something strong would give him some ideas.

CHAPTER 9

Act like a Soldier

Jake trudged through what used to be their camp, looking for a way he could help the battalion pull itself back together. Nothing presented itself—nothing for a mech to help with, anyway.

Everything that had been broken was broken, and both his giant hands and his vast arsenal had been designed for destruction, not rebuilding. Beth, Tommy, Richaud, and Ash had already extracted the remaining quad from the ruined personnel carrier, affixing it to the top of one of the tanks.

Now, it seemed, there was nothing left for the **MIMAS** mechs to do except to remain alert and on guard, patrolling to protect what had already been stolen.

I failed.

There was no escaping that fact. Jake had been the one to spot the one-eared Quatro making for the personnel carriers—the others had been busy fighting for their lives. Circumstances had assigned *him* with the task of making sure the Quatro didn't manage to access one of the quads. But he'd failed. And now, all of Eresos was at risk.

"Price." It was Roach, subvocalizing.

"Sir?"

"Get over here."

Jake's HUD flashed with Roach's location, a hundred meters or so past the camp's perimeter, well within the trees.

How'd he end up there without anyone noticing?

With the mech's long legs and its unrivaled locomotion, he reached Roach in less than a minute, even though he had to jog around the camp to avoid running over anyone, and then he had to weave through the trees to avoid knocking one of those down and making a racket—never a welcome outcome, especially in the wake of a Quatro attack.

He found Roach sitting on a thick, fallen tree. From the looks of the stump, Roach had cracked the thing off to serve as his mech's seat. It was odd to see the great war machine in repose.

Jake saluted. "You wanted to speak with me, sir?" He decided not to ask why Roach had risked straying so far from the camp. Lately, he'd been trying not to question his superior.

"I want you to take command of Oneiri Team and push on toward Ingress."

For a moment, Jake didn't know what to say to that. "Sir...take command? Plenty of people in the reserve battalion outrank me, and a lot of the garrison soldiers do, too." He wasn't sure why that was the first point he raised, but there it was.

"They can sort themselves out," Gabe said. "But they don't understand mechs, and I don't want them directing you to do anything. I'll transmit signed orders to that effect."

"I take it this means you're leaving."

"Good deduction. I intend to track down the Quatro that stole that quad, and when I find it, I mean to disable it. Do not follow me, and make sure the others don't, either. That's an order, Price. I want you to impress that on the others. An *order*, damn it. I'll be blocking my transponder from broadcasting my location to you, but I hope that's an unnecessary measure."

"Sir, do you really think you need to deny us knowledge of your location? I mean, we won't follow you, but if you run into trouble—"

"Damn it, Price, this is exactly why I need to block my transponder. You were about to say that if something happens to me, you'd come try to pull me out of it, and that's what I just ordered you *not* to do." Roach's mech was shaking its head. "Typical."

"Sir...why choose *me* to command Oneiri? I failed. I let the Quatro steal the quad."

Roach surged to his feet, crossing the distance between him and Jake in an instant, so that their faces were inches away. Even though Jake was also inside a giant robot, Roach still managed to be intimidating.

"Is this the result of your training, Seaman Apprentice? Did I teach you to mope around when the going gets tough, or did I teach you to act like a soldier?"

"The latter, sir."

"Then act like one! That's an order, too."

"Sir...why do you think the Quatro retreated? Why not press the advantage, once they had the quad?"

"They were taking heavy losses. If the battle had gone on much longer, most of them would probably be dead. But they have the quad, now, and they'll learn the thing's power, the extent of which we're not even sure about. They could do a lot of damage with it."

Jake nodded. Ever since the Siege of Plenitos had begun, the chief had been exhibiting signs of exhaustion and mental instability. He'd screwed up the launch that had brought them wide of the Quatro force besieging Plenitos, which had resulted in the enemy breaching the walls. Shortly after that, Jake had found him standing on the edge of the woods, motionless, staring at the fractured city.

And now, he was heading alone into the wilderness, to chase a weapon whose capabilities he knew nothing about.

But Jake had resolved not to question the chief.

"It's possible I'll find the Quatro dead inside the quad it took," Roach said. "The mech your father found in that comet killed Zimmerman when he couldn't control it. But I have to make sure. Do you understand that, Price?"

"Yes, sir."

"Good. Now, get those quads to Ingress. Don't let me down."

With that, Roach turned and walked into the woods. Jake watched him until the trees blocked him out, and then he listened until the sound of Roach's mech crashing through the undergrowth faded away.

CHAPTER 10

Played

"Don't tell me," Former Habitat 2 councilman Leonardo Fiore said as he sneered at Lisa through the bars of his cell. "Are you going to offer me leniency in exchange for information? We all know how *that* turned out."

The former councilman was tall, lithe, and tanned. The kind of tan that was difficult to attain inside a sealed habitat, without spending ample time lying in a tanning bed.

"Actually, I haven't decided what I should offer you," Lisa said, returning Fiore's gaze without breaking eye contact. "What did Quentin Cooper offer you, that made you spill your guts so liberally?"

"Oh, I'm confident he'll find a way to reward me. I'm a man with...broad tastes." Fiore's eyes slithered up and down Lisa's body, which made her feel like vomiting.

Refusing to let her nausea show, Lisa continued to study the man's lean face.

She knew what her father would say about a man like Fiore: his overconfidence blinded him to his own shortcomings. It was easy to find that sort of man's buttons, and once you found them, it was even easier to jam your thumb down on them till he behaved exactly as you wanted.

"I'm afraid he won't get the chance to reward you," Lisa said. "Darkstream is deploying an entire battalion of trained soldiers to Habitat 2. Cooper doesn't have a prayer of victory. He's already enjoyed all the success he's going to."

"You're a fool, girl," Fiore spat, and Lisa didn't react to that either, despite how much she hated being called "girl" after months trapped inside a beetle with Tessa Notaras. "Cooper's spent *years* preparing for this. You've done nothing but set him back a little. He has sprawling facilities that he built years ago, inside hills well outside the beetle routes. *I* helped him do that. I used my position on the council to redirect what resources I could to him, and I was repaid in kind. Plus, Cooper has soldiers of his own, armed with weaponry *I* helped him to secure, and beetles built with parts that *I* procured for him. How else do you explain the sheer volume of drugs that flooded not just this habitat, but all of the habitats? Cooper's operation is not some two-bit racket. It spans the planet, with operatives in every habitat, as well as inside Darkstream's own power structure. Those operatives will be on their way, soon. You're *done,* girl. Done."

Lisa nodded, saying nothing. By bruising Fiore's pride, she'd prompted him to give her exactly what she wanted, and it had been almost as easy as pushing "play" on a vid using her implant.

Of course, to tell Fiore he'd been played would put him on guard against the tactic in the future, and she wanted to preserve it, in case she ever needed it again.

So she maintained her silence as she exited the cell block, which she knew would likely make him think his words had had the impact he'd wanted.

"Do visit again," Fiore shouted after her. "It would be my pleasure to *educate* you as much as is needed."

As Lisa returned to her office, she received a message from the council of Habitat 1, notifying her that their entire fleet of beetles had been stolen.

That was as good as confirmation of Fiore's boasting.

So he was telling the truth. Cooper really is coming.

"Let him come," she muttered to the empty room. "We'll be ready and waiting."

CHAPTER 11

Vaguely Humanoid

"Another day, another comet, eh boss?" Ellis Green said with his easy grin. "You want me to double check your pressure suit?"

"The computer should have it covered." Peter Price had once been a lot more diligent about manually checking over the suit's seals. That had been when his son had worked with him, and he'd wanted to instill good habits.

I should still be that diligent.

Jake might not be here, but Sue Anne was still counting on him, and it wouldn't help her if he died because he'd been negligent about his pressure suit.

All the same, he didn't ask Ellis to check it. Instead, he stepped inside the airlock and waited for the man to join him.

"Where's Noah?" Peter asked as the inner door sealed.

Ellis's eyes flitted away before returning to meet Peter's once more. "He said he'd be right out."

"Uh huh." *Slept in again.*

"What do you think we'll find inside this ice ball, boss?"

It was a joke. Peter hadn't found anything unusual since he'd uncovered the mech with his son, which had turned out to be a tremendous windfall. Darkstream had paid him two billion credits for his share of the find, and he'd used the money to lease another comet hopper from Darkstream, and to hire two men and three women to help him increase the number of comets he could turn into homes each year. After a few months, he'd made enough credits to lease a third.

In exchange for all that, he'd allowed Darkstream to take his son away from him. To go kill Quatro on the surface of Eresos, millions of miles away.

To lose his soul.

He tried to return Ellis's grin, with one of his own. It felt halfhearted on his lips. "There's only one way to know what we'll find," he said as the outer hatch opened to let them out onto the ice. "We just have to find it."

He knew Ellis was only trying to build up a rapport with him. The three of them had to live together, after all, in fairly close quarters. It got lonely out here in the Belt, far away from the inner system, and far away from Hub, the Belt's only real city.

But part of Peter still didn't want to accept that he'd lost the dynamic he'd had out here with his son, and that he'd never get it back. There'd been something special about there just being the two of them, going it alone against space and ice, carving out a living, as well as enough money to pay for Sue Anne's medical treatment.

He was sure Jake had never enjoyed the experience as much as he had. Most likely, Peter was just as foolish as any father who tried overzealously to share his passion with his son.

That didn't change the fact he missed Jake dearly.

He walked around the comet hopper, which Jake had always called the *Whale*, and now Peter did, too. He reached the compartment that housed the half-kilometer coiled drilling hose.

By now, Ellis didn't need to be told what to do. He approached a panel near the bow of the ship, which extended outward to reveal the antenna array. That done, Ellis would instruct the array to use step-frequency radar to scan the comet, so they'd know what they were in for in terms of the ice's density.

"Noah," Peter said, using his radio to broadcast his voice throughout the *Whale*. "Have you activated the water harvester?"

"I will now," came the reply, and Peter rolled his eyes before returning to the task of preparing the hose to blast the comet with boiling water.

At least, I'll blast it with boiling water eventually.

Because Noah was so late in getting started on his part of the job, it would be some time before the water harvester collected and heated enough liquid to begin drilling.

"Boss," Ellis said. From his gestures, Peter could tell he'd been reviewing the radar scan's findings, but his hand had paused in midair. "The scan found something."

"Is that another joke?"

"No. Seriously. Just a few meters below the surface. Take a look at this."

Ellis made the flicking gesture that would transmit an image to Peter's HUD, but before it rendered, something *emerged* from the comet, breaking through the ice and crawling out onto the surface.

As it got to its feet, it was vaguely humanoid, though it wasn't much higher than Peter's belly button. That said, it seemed to hunch slightly, gleaming dully in the dim light.

The thing had dark gray, metallic arms like elongated shields, and its thighs and shins had the same shape, only shorter. Peter couldn't discern a face anywhere on its elongated head, which extended forward as well as backward. The thing didn't even seem to have any eyes, or sensors of any kind. None that were evident, anyway.

Without warning, the machine's arms snapped downward against the ice, sending it sailing off into space with startling speed—deeper into the Belt.

"What *was* that thing?" Ellis asked, his voice filled with awe.

"I have no idea," Peter said. "But I'd better go back inside. Darkstream will want to know about this right away."

"You really think you'll be able to sell this one too, boss?" Ellis asked, jocularity already creeping back into his voice. "I mean, it got away, didn't it?"

But Peter didn't answer. Suddenly, he felt even less receptive toward Ellis's jokes than he'd been before.

CHAPTER 12

Militia

"It's interesting that Daybreak didn't position any snipers up here," Lisa said, her pressure suit's audio picking up her own footfalls across Habitat 2's gunmetal gray roof.

Ahead of her, Tessa shrugged her slim shoulders. "Doesn't surprise me, honestly. I doubt Daybreak expected to be attacked. They were negotiating with Darkstream, and other than the company, who would have the resources to oppose them?"

"Us."

"Us and the Quatro. Who no one knew were even on Alex. Besides, we lured them into the valley, which a rooftop sniper wouldn't have been able to hit anyway."

Lisa didn't answer. As always, Tessa's tactical analysis was dead-on, but that didn't mean she needed to be praised endlessly for it.

She's confident enough as it is.

If only Tessa had been able to appraise Darkstream just as accurately. Lisa had a lot of affection for Tessa, but the woman's hatred for Darkstream made their friendship a little strained at times.

"Andy's been talking you up, lately," the former soldier said, turning so Lisa could glimpse her amused expression through her faceplate. "Says he's impressed with everything you've accomplished, this last little while. I do believe the boy is growing smitten with you."

Lisa offered a terse chuckle. "If he is, it won't be for long. Andy's as fickle as a pickle."

"How fickle is a pickle, exactly?"

Shaking her head, Lisa grinned to herself as they reached the edge of the roof and she gazed out over Alex's blue expanse. "Just a cheesy saying my dad used to trot out way too much."

Dust devils chased each other across the terrain, putting on a little performance for the two friends. After long months cooped up in a beetle, with nothing to look at but this, Lisa would have thought she'd have tired of the planet's beauty.

Not so. And, watching more loose shapes of dust form and dissipate, over and over, she doubted she ever would.

Tessa turned to her. "Unlike Cooper, we have the advantage of having advance notice of the coming attack. We *can* put snipers up here."

"Yeah. Although, they'll be most effective if we can anticipate what direction they'll hit us from. Otherwise, we'll have to allow time for our snipers to move across the roof. Which might take too long for them to have any effect at all."

Tessa sniffed. "Shouldn't be hard to anticipate where Cooper will hit. We can just keep an eye on the satellite images—providing Darkstream allows us continued access to them."

For the second time today, Lisa responded to her friend with only silence.

The older woman sighed. "I know how fond you are of your employer, Lisa. But whether I'm right about them or not, I hope you realize that we can't leave the safety of Habitat 2 up to the timing of their arrival. If they take their sweet time to get here...well, I don't need to spell it out, do I?"

"I've already thought about that, Tessa. And I agree." Her friend did have a point. The charge that Darkstream's bureaucracy could be slow and cumbersome held a *lot* of water. "I'm going to start training a citizen militia. Providing the council approves, obviously." A new city council had just been elected by the habitat's residents, and Lisa had no intention of subverting them. "I think they'll approve it. Darkstream won't like it, but Habitat 2 is too important to leave its fate to chance."

Through Tessa's faceplate, Lisa could see that her eyebrows were hiked up as far as they would go. "You surprise me more every day, Lisa. I honestly didn't expect to hear you say that. Not without a lot of convincing."

"Well, don't expect me to start endorsing your crazy theories just yet. This is strictly about pragmatism."

Tessa smiled. "I'm choosing to see it as a sign there's some hope for you."

"Yeah, yeah. Think we'll get Andy firing a gun and shooting straight?"

"He won't be *thinking* straight enough to shoot straight. Not with you around." Then, Tessa's smile turned down a couple notches. "You know, Daybreak did leave a few Three Points members alive."

Lisa tilted her head to the side. "Wow, Tessa. Really? Are you really about to say what I think you are?"

"There's no one who hates Daybreak more than them."

"Out of the question. They're staying in their cells, and they certainly aren't joining any militia. The council would never sign off on it, for one."

Tessa turned from the edge of the roof and started back toward the nearest airlock leading down into Habitat 2. "Well, here's hoping recruitment goes well for you. If it doesn't, and Daybreak shows up with Darkstream still nowhere in sight, you may find yourself singing a different tune."

CHAPTER 13

Not Just a War of Expansion

Whatever else was true about the quad the Quatro had stolen, tracking it did not offer much of a challenge.

That was because it apparently had the power to obliterate trees, leaving only splintered stumps and a shower of bark. The MIMAS mechs could do that to smaller trees, at a full run. Gabe had no idea how fast the quad was moving, but the wreckage it left in its path...

Suffice it to say I'd rather it didn't do that to my mech.

Despite his growing trepidation, it brought him a measure of relief to do something other than fight in a battle.

Killing had never been a problem for him before, but since the start of this war, it tended to cause him paralyzing, guilt-ridden flashbacks of the first missions on Eresos, to subdue the Quatro population.

He didn't know why it was flashbacks of killing aliens and not fellow humans that haunted him, but he didn't pretend to know how the human brain worked.

The one thing he was certain of was that chasing the quad did not seem to trigger any flashbacks. He welcomed the reprieve.

Then, he started seeing Jess.

He was loping along the swath of destruction the quad had left in its wake when she appeared right in the middle of it. Her arms were folded across her stomach, and her auburn hair shifted in the breeze.

Gabe twisted to the right, trying to change his course, but he only succeeded in losing his balance, crashing forward. If Jess had been real, he would have crushed her.

But the MIMAS passed through nothing, and he hit the ground hard, the dream translating the mech's impact as a wave of pain that spread through Gabe's body.

He pulled himself to his feet and checked all around him, but there was no sign of Jess, other than his racing heartbeat, which manifested inside the dream as a shimmer over everything in his sight.

The dream.

It was only supposed to make people appear like that when Gabe was communicating with them, to provide the illusion of an in-person conversation, which was supposed to improve the quality of long-distance meetings.

It was also supposed to only show him people who still lived.

But Jess did not live. He'd seen her body with his own eyes, after the Quatro attacked Northshire, which he'd been assigned to protect.

She was the reason he'd embarked on this war in the first place. It wasn't just Darkstream's war of expansion; it was also his own war of personal vengeance, and for Gabe, the second came before the first.

And now here Jess was, to...what? Cheer him on?

He didn't think so. He didn't think she was here to do anything.

She hadn't been there at all, of course—not really. It was just the mech dream conspiring with his increasingly unstable subconscious to unsettle him.

It was also a reminder, an affirmation, that he really would stop at nothing to secure his vengeance. He wouldn't even be stopped by the dead girl he was striving to avenge.

Gabe resumed his headlong dash through the forest, determined not to rest until he caught up to the quad. No matter what happened next.

CHAPTER 14

Extermination Is Also Acceptable

The Quatro had proved themselves formidable warriors during the Battle for Habitat 2, and they were willing to help again in its defense.

But according to Fiore's boasting, Lisa would need more than just the Quatro to defend her home.

And so, she put out the call to all residents of Habitat 2 interested in fighting Daybreak—anyone who wanted to prevent their home from being taken once again by ruthless criminals were told to meet her in the central plaza at six AM.

She got five people.

Tessa Notaras, Andy Miller, Bob O'Toole, Phineas Gage, and a red-haired man named Rodney Vickers, who Lisa was pretty sure just wanted an excuse to play with explosives.

"Um, do you think it's the early hour?" Andy asked, scratching his head through his brown hair.

Lisa frowned. "For the opportunity to defend your home, the time of day shouldn't matter."

Presumably, no one wanted to become slaves to Daybreak again. But apparently, they assumed that period of oppression had been just a momentary blip, an anomaly, which couldn't possibly happen again now that a Darkstream military operative had taken care of the situation and more operatives were on the way.

The residents of Habitat 2 clearly felt that someone else would handle things, and that they could simply return to their normal lives.

"Well," Lisa said, "I guess we'll make do with what we have, for now. Who knows, if we all work hard, maybe we'll inspire others to join us." She cleared her throat. "Okay. First things first. I thought we'd start by putting on pressure suits and going out on Alex for some real-life shooting. I know you've all probably fired a gun before, in lucid, and maybe even during your waking life, but we'll mostly be training in the latter. There's nothing like firing a real gun. Someone I have a lot of respect for once told me that." Exchanging smiles with Tessa, Lisa said, "All right. Everyone make for the western airlock."

As they reentered Habitat 2's narrow streets, Lisa drew up beside Tessa and said, "You're not really going to let me train you, are you? You know way more than me. Plus, you have way more actual battle experience."

"Consider me here in an observation capacity," Tessa said. "I trained you how to fight, and how to endure the rigors of combat. I didn't teach you how to train others. So I'm interested to see how you make out." Tessa shrugged. "Besides, it never hurts to brush up on fundamentals."

"Fair enough." Lisa chuckled. "I guess I can get you to take over, too, in case I need to use the washroom."

She'd just started to put on her pressure suit when her HUD notified her that she had an urgent message.

It was Commander Laudano. "Seaman Sato. A subordinate has forwarded me a link to a system net news site, and I found what I saw there deeply disturbing. Unless these photos are doctored, it would seem you have *Quatro* freely roaming the streets of Habitat 2. I find it curious that you failed to include their presence in any of your reports. Worse, according to this news site, you *arrived* with these creatures. Now, I have no idea how the Quatro are even *on* Alex, but what I do know is that the species is responsible for thousands of deaths on Eresos and counting. Clearly, they're far more advanced than we've dared to consider. How they traveled from Eresos to Alex is beyond me, especially considering no unidentified traffic has been detected between the two planets. Maybe they've discovered a way to open up some sort of quantum tunnel between their caves on Eresos and on Alex. Either way, I'm willing to give you the benefit of the doubt and assume that these beasts have tricked you somehow. But that benefit only extends so far. If you'd like to continual availing of it, I highly recommend you apprehend every Quatro currently inside Habitat 2. Exterminating them will also be acceptable. Laudano out."

"I have to go," Lisa said, dropping the pieces of her pressure suit. "Tessa, if you could take over for me?"

Her friend nodded, and Lisa ran back into Habitat 2. By the time she found Rug, she was completely out of breath. The alien was doing what she always did: pacing the streets of the city, completely ignoring its inhabitants.

"Rug," Lisa managed through her panting. "You have to leave. It isn't safe for you here anymore."

Rug regarded her with large midnight eyes. Those eyes always seemed so calm, and they still did now, reflecting none of the anxiety Lisa was experiencing. "Why do you say so, human?"

"I just heard from one of my Darkstream bosses. He ordered me to either arrest you, or...or *exterminate* you. I have to assume the Darkstream soldiers in transit to here will know I've been given those orders, but either way, I doubt they'll react to your presence positively. I have no idea when they're going to get here. They could arrive within the hour. I'm not about to let any harm come to you or your people, Rug. I refuse to. Especially after everything you've done to help us."

"And I refuse to abandon you to Daybreak, Lisa. I know that the others of my drift will feel the same."

"You don't understand, Rug. You must leave."

"No, Lisa. You misunderstand me. We *will* leave Habitat 2. But we will not go far. My drift will remain nearby, and when Quentin Cooper returns to try to take from you what is rightfully yours, we will strike him with the full extent of our fury. That is not open to negotiation."

Lisa felt a smile break over her face, and she surprised them both by reaching up to wrap her arms around the large alien. Rug seemed to take it in stride.

"Thank you, Rug."

CHAPTER 15

Operational Details

The Darkstream soldiers finally arrived, and they didn't bother to notify Lisa until their shuttles were landing on the roof of Habitat 2.

She quickly assembled a welcoming party, consisting of her, most of the new council, and some of the habitat's prominent business leaders, including her friend Phineas Gage.

She even included Candace Peele, owner of the Swinging Eel, whose clientele had once consisted mostly of Daybreak and Three Points members. Peele herself had never been found guilty of anything, and the Swinging Eel had fallen on hard times since Quentin Cooper's defeat.

Peele was currently in the midst of a halfhearted rebranding, but sometimes Lisa suspected she was quietly rooting for Cooper to return and take over Habitat 2 once more.

The freight elevator from Habitat 2's roof opened, and a squad's worth of soldiers poured out. Lisa was surprised to see that Mario Laudano was one of them.

She marched forward, drawing to a halt in front of him and stomping her right foot perfectly in line with her left, coming to attention. Her right hand snapped up to her temple in a crisp salute. "Welcome to Habitat 2, sir. I was not aware that you planned to personally lead the battalion."

Laudano returned her salute, his much sloppier than hers, as though he found the exercise tiresome. "Ranking Darkstream security personnel don't typically make a habit of keeping seamen appraised of every little operational detail."

Well, this seaman happens to have saved this city. She didn't say that, though. "Yes, sir. Where are the rest of your soldiers?"

Laudano's mouth twisted slightly. "They'll be down shortly."

And so they were. Ten shuttles had made their way from Valhalla, carrying a sizable force.

Things changed rapidly, after their arrival.

For one, Laudano's people were even more standoffish than the Quatro had been toward humans who weren't Lisa, Tessa, or Andy.

The Darkstream operatives marched the streets stiffly, in full uniform and carrying heavy artillery everywhere they went. Like the Quatro, they did not stop or make way for anyone else, instead claiming the right-of-way everywhere they went.

Lisa's workload diminished drastically, which was a welcome change. However, the work she did find herself doing was much less interesting than investigating and prosecuting Daybreak, or helping the new council get accustomed to their administrative duties.

On his third day in Habitat 2, Laudano offered to renew Darkstream's old contract with the council at a cut-rate price. It was an offer too good to refuse.

Not long after, Laudano approached Lisa in a jet-black pressure suit as she was training her militia out on Alex, in the evening hours after she got off work.

The militia had more than tripled in size since she'd started it. That only amounted to sixteen members total, but they'd come a long way, and she was proud of them.

That ended today, apparently.

"What is this?" Laudano barked over a wide channel, so that all of Lisa's militia men and women could hear.

Hesitating, Lisa indicated her soldiers with a spread hand. "These people want to help defend their homes when Quentin Cooper comes for it."

"I just brought an entire Darkstream reserve battalion for that purpose."

"I realize that, sir...but the more fighters we have, the greater our chance of victory will be."

Laudano shook his head back and forth vigorously. "Our chance of victory already rests at one hundred percent. As you well know, Darkstream soldiers are highly trained, and mine are some of the most battle-hardened in the entire company."

I'm not sure Tessa would agree with that assessment. Indeed, the ex-soldier stood stiffly nearby, glaring at Laudano through her faceplate.

The commander didn't seem to notice. "Speaking of which, Darkstream did not invest tens of thousands of credits in training you, Seaman Sato, so that you could give away that training for free. You are to desist immediately. That's an order."

"But, sir—"

"One more word, and I'll mark you for disciplinary action. I'm not one who stands for having his orders questioned. Not in the slightest."

"Yes, sir."

With that, Laudano spun neatly on his heel and marched back toward Habitat 2.

"I don't trust *that* at all," Tessa said, and Lisa's HUD told her she spoke over a two-way channel.

"Neither do I." She couldn't quite put her finger on it, but the fact that Laudano would want to stop her from increasing residents' ability to defend themselves seemed very odd. It reminded her of the way the commander had insisted on the arrest of the Quatro, even though the aliens had helped retake Habitat 2, which should have been obvious to anyone with a system net connection.

Laudano still hadn't asked what had become of the Quatro, and Lisa wondered whether he would. Maybe he had chosen to assume she had actually killed them, but wasn't interested in dealing with the paperwork that would result from discovering that she had.

She opened up a wide channel with the members of her militia—one that excluded Laudano, who still hadn't reached Habitat 2 yet.

"You heard the commander. I'm going to have to stop using Darkstream resources in order to train you." That hadn't been exactly what Laudano said, but the interpretation suited her purposes. "So I guess we're just going to have to continue our training in lucid, aren't we? I'm sending you the code for a meeting lobby now. In the meantime, I suggest you all go perform some 'non-training related PT' with Tessa, so that she can ensure your implants are calibrated to accurately reflect your physical abilities. Just as a favor to you, of course—nothing to do with our militia." Lisa smiled at them. "I'll see you all tonight."

CHAPTER 16

Eyes Aglow

Gabe took pride in the fact that, the next time Jess appeared to him, he managed to keep his composure.

This time, she wasn't standing directly in his path. Instead, he spotted her on a low hill to the right of the swath left behind by the quad. He almost missed her, in fact. That notion struck him as incredibly bizarre.

Imagine missing your own hallucination.

Would it still be hallucinating if you didn't even notice your delusions?

It was a question for another time. For now, he stopped amidst the downed and splintered trees, staring at her and keeping his mech's hands by its sides.

"Why are you running?" Jess said, in the same matter-of-fact fashion she'd always said...well, pretty much everything.

Gabe didn't answer.

She looks just as beautiful as the day we...

No. More beautiful. Her beauty was increased by the fact he missed her so much.

"Are you running toward something? Or *from* something?"

"Toward," Gabe said.

"I say from. And I think I'm right. So now that we've determined that, the only thing that's left is to find out what it is you're running from. Could it be the Quatro whose air you turned to fire under the orders of your employer?"

"Jess. Please."

"You didn't even give them the chance to fight, did you? You incinerated them in their homes. Is that how a soldier behaves?"

"Yes."

"Maybe I'm wrong about what you're running from. What do I know? I do like guessing, though. Let me guess again. Maybe you're still running from the Bastion Sector, back in the Milky Way. I was born in the Milky Way, just like you. But I only spent a couple of years there. I didn't get the chance to see the things you saw. To do the things you did."

Gabe didn't speak, having already gained the sense that doing so would only make things worse. That had often been the way, with Jess.

"Are you running from the boy you found, after UHF bombs destroyed the radicals' base on Thessaly? He begged you to kill him, didn't he? He was gone below the waist, completely gone, and he was bleeding out, but it was taking a long time. There was no saving him. Probably. Either way, he begged you to kill him, and you did it. Didn't you?"

Everything in the world had turned various shades of blue. A MIMAS mech could not weep, but the dream did turn everything blue.

"Have you forgotten about the boy, Gabe? Have other horrors replaced his memory?"

A strong wind picked up, causing the sapphire trees to sway.

"I'm glad to have reminded you about him," Jess said. "He seemed like he was probably a nice boy, all things considered. And he was even younger than *I* was when I died."

Jess vanished, and at the same time, the woods regained their normal colors. Gabe was alone again.

He resumed running.

It was beginning to get dark. But something made him feel like he was getting close. The woods were thickening, and judging by the slightly reduced length of the quad's strides, as indicated by its tracks, it had been slowed by it. Not by much, but some.

Gabe was not slowed. His path had been cleared by the quad's labor, and soon he would catch up.

Then, I'll kill it. For Jess.

The woods ended with an abruptness that clearly wasn't natural. Someone had cleared a wide space, for defensive purposes.

Indeed, a tiny cluster of structures lay in the middle of the cleared area. When Gabe consulted his map, this wasn't on it. That meant mercenaries.

The thought didn't stop him. Nothing but death would, now – he'd resolved that long ago.

Instead of stopping, he charged faster, intending to take anyone who remained in that ramshackle settlement by surprise.

But it was he who was taken by surprise.

The buildings were arranged in a rough circle, and in their center stood the quad, its eyes aglow in the waning light.

MIMAS mechs were much taller than Quatro, but inside its own mech, the alien came almost to the shoulders of Gabe's.

It made no move toward him, and Gabe did what he could to arrest his own momentum, catching himself on the side of a shed, which caused the wood to splinter, buckle inward, and crack.

Twin cannons formed to flank the quad's head, pointing straight at Gabe.

He leapt to his left.

CHAPTER 17

Feedback Mechanism

Gabe tucked into a roll as a blast of energy made a crater where he'd been standing. The quad turned to fire on him again, but he was still moving, speeding up, and the shot only succeeded in catching another wooden structure ablaze.

Ducking behind a third structure, he paused for a second to gather his wits and attempt to formulate some kind of plan. But the Quatro piloting the quad clearly had no intention of giving him any time for that. It fired again, this time with what seemed like armor-piercing rounds, against which the building Gabe hid behind offered basically no protection.

A round caught his arm, denting it and flinging it backward. Another hit his shoulder, causing him to spin. He turned into the revolution and fled once more, retracting his hands against his wrists and spinning up both auto cannons to fire on his enemy as he did.

The Quatro was completely undeterred. It ran straight into the hail of bullets, the ordnance making pinging sounds as it glanced off of the quad's armor.

Steeling himself, Gabe squared up to meet the charge, bracing himself by shifting his right foot back and bringing both hands up before him, metal fingers spread to catch the beast.

The quad simply trampled him, heavy paws knocking him down and pummeling him into the earth.

He cried out in agony as the dream tried to convince him that his body was shattered beyond repair, bones ground to dust, organs ruptured like overfilled balloons.

Maybe that feedback mechanism is a little too *intense.* Or maybe his body really was destroyed.

Deciding to do what he could to test the hypothesis, he pushed himself to his feet, forcing himself to run at his foe, who was coming about to charge again.

This time, Gabe was ready. With a mighty leap, he sailed over the quad, pelting it with his autocannons all the while.

A weapon that closely resembled a rocket launcher took shape from the metal on the quad's back, and indeed a rocket emerged from it, timed to catch Gabe at the peak of his jump. The missile scored a direct hit with his right side, and the explosion threw him farther into the air, limbs flailing uncontrollably.

As Gabe descended, the quad's tail took the shape of a great blade poised to skewer him on the way down.

It was possible that the **MIMAS** mech's armor was strong enough to withstand being run through, even with its full weight coming down on a single wicked-looking point.

But Gabe wasn't eager to test *that*. Instead, he fired every rocket he had in his arsenal in the quad's direction. The effort served to stabilize his descent somewhat, and he turned his auto cannons on the alien once more as he finished falling.

The kickback from his firing served to push him backward slightly, and he missed the blade by a matter of centimeters.

Extending his own blades, Gabe drove them forward into the quad's armor, producing a piercing shriek of metal against metal. His effort produced only thin, white lines, like those made by a butter knife across a wooden table top.

The Quatro spun, swinging a massive paw at Gabe's head in a gesture reminiscent of the one that had killed Tommy deep underground. Gabe felt sure he had time to dodge, but he was wrong. The blow knocked him to the ground, where he rolled sideways to avoid whatever the Quatro was planning next.

Gabe regained his feet, but immediately a blast of energy threw him straight through another structure. He landed inside, his entire body on fire.

The quad came in after him, landing on top of him, raking him with razor claws that had formed the moment the Quatro had need of them. Furrows of pain sprang up all down Gabe's body.

He let two grenades tumble out of his grenade launchers, without actually launching them. Both exploded, causing Gabe's anguish to spike brutally but forcing the Quatro to ease up enough for him to scramble out from underneath it.

Charging at one of the unbroken walls, he succeeded in breaking through to the outside.

There, he came face to face with a group of two dozen mercenaries, bearing all manner of artillery. They stood approximately thirty meters away.

Two of them directed rocket launchers at Gabe and fired.

CHAPTER 18

Creative Karma

Another energy blast followed him between the trees as he attempted to flee into the rapidly darkening woods.

The dry, leafless trees all around him exploded into flame, and Gabe pitched forward, face-first into the forest floor.

He staggered once more to his feet, a rocket sailing past him to hit an unusually large tree, which the explosion enveloped. Gabe stumbled around it, though the heat found him, spurring him to run as quickly as he could.

His mech was behaving erratically. He suspected the fight had done serious damage to the actuators and servomotors in several of his joints, as he was having great difficulty in making the MIMAS go where he wanted it to.

An attempt to sprint between two trees resulted in colliding with the leftmost one, causing him to spin and almost lose his balance again. He found his feet, somehow, and staggered on, the shouts of the mercenaries close behind him, their bullets ripping up the ground all around him.

Make for the densest cluster of trees. That's your only hope.

Gabe did. It was almost night, and he prayed his pursuers would lose track of him...if he could just keep moving.

His HUD had been nagging him to review his vitals, but he hadn't found the time for it in between running for his life. While the dream interface granted him an incredibly close connection with his mech, it distanced himself from his own body.

He reached a part of the woods where the trees grew close together, and he weaved through them as best he could, hoping they would slow the quad some. Only then did he glance at what his implant was trying to tell him about his body's health.

The prognosis wasn't good. He was slowly bleeding out, just like the boy back on Thessaly had been, and if he didn't get medical attention soon, he would die, just as the boy had.

That wasn't an acceptable outcome, he decided. The other members of Oneiri team had to be warned of the devastating power wielded by the quad, as well as the fact he'd found it in a mercenary outpost.

Were those Red Company fighters?

He had no way of knowing, other than a massive hunch. Another hunch told him there was a reason the Quatro who'd stolen the quad had gone to the mercenaries. It had headed straight for their settlement, and Gabe seriously doubted that was by chance.

It thought it had something to gain there.

That meant the Quatro almost certainly had an alliance with the mercenaries, or some sort of arrangement, at least. If Darkstream's enemies were uniting against the company, then that was a piece of information that gravely needed to be passed on as well.

If only he believed that he actually had a chance of making it back to his team.

As he ran, he briefly considered allowing his transponder to broadcast his location to Price and the others, so that they could come to his aid. But he quickly scrapped it as a horrible idea.

The fact that he hadn't encountered any Quatro other than the one piloting the quad told him the other aliens had likely continued to trail the Darkstream battalion, looking for a chance to strike and liberate more of the quads. Even if that wasn't the case, the quad had made short work of him, and he wasn't totally confident that even the combined might of Oneiri team could take it down. True, it had taken the arrival of the mercenaries to finish Gabe off, but he didn't know how long he would've lasted against the quad even in their absence.

It would've taken dying in a one-on-one duel with the quad to get a more accurate impression of its prowess, but that would not have served anyone.

He passed Jess as he barreled through the dense wood. She was standing between two trees that left a gap much too narrow for his mech to fit between.

"Do you believe in karma?" she asked, but by the time his overtaxed brain registered the question, he was already too far to answer her.

Then he saw her again, standing at the bottom of a natural bowl in a small clearing dead ahead.

"If karma does exist, I wonder what its limits might be?"

Again, Gabe rushed past too quickly to engage in any conversation, let alone one about complex philosophical issues.

But then, Jess reappeared just ahead. "If someone's committed an excessive number of horrible acts," she said, "how can karma possibly compensate for that?"

Gabe stumbled on, but this time Jess shrieked loud enough for him to hear: "How creative is karma willing to get?"

As Gabe continued on through the woods, the gunfire and explosions grew dimmer behind him. He wasn't sure whether that was because he was succeeding in putting distance between him and his pursuers, or because he was losing consciousness.

He gradually became obsessed with the concept of blood loss, and the dream facilitated that obsession. Droplets of blood started to ooze from every tree, and pools of it welled up from the ground.

The sky itself began to bleed.

CHAPTER 19

Sucker for Punishment

"See you tomorrow night," Bob O'Toole said, peering at Lisa.

Lisa grunted, and he vanished.

Tessa grinned. "That's the one circumstance where he'll ever get to say that and it'll be true." Then she disappeared too, leaving just Lisa and Andy in the lucid lobby.

Since Laudano had disbanded it, Lisa's militia had almost doubled in size. Nothing quite got the word out like having a secret group that no one else was meant to know about, she supposed.

She turned most of their lucid simulations down to minimum lucidity, so that her trainees forgot entirely that they were dreaming for the duration of the dream, convinced the sims were real life and that they truly were in danger.

At the end of each sim, however, they were all sent to a lobby with the lucidity turned up to max so that they could review whatever scenario they'd just run—what had worked, who had died, and what might have gone better.

They'd just conducted tonight's final scenario, though she wished there were more. She found it incredibly rewarding to watch her charges improve.

They'd been doing that a lot, lately. Improving. Especially since they'd begun training entirely in lucid. Dream-time was incredibly condensed. One minute of real-time could equal fifteen minutes of dream-time, often more. That meant they were able to get at least fifteen times the amount of training in.

Daybreak won't stand a chance.

"I feel like tonight went great," Andy said.

Lisa nodded. "They've all been going great. Everyone has their basics down pat, so now we can finally begin to innovate."

"Yeah." Andy rubbed the back of his neck, which must've been a gesture of discomfort, considering it was unlikely he would dream he had an itch in full lucidity. He met her eyes. "Listen, do you feel like getting a drink together soon? Tomorrow, maybe?"

That took her aback. "Um, yeah! Sure. I get off at eight in the evening. So, maybe nine? Dusty Bucket?"

"Sounds good! See you then." With that, Andy winked out of existence.

Before returning to her regular sleep, Lisa took a moment to process that. If she was being honest with herself, and she saw no reason not to be, she was excited by the attention from Andy. But it also made her wonder—why the sudden interest now?

Nevertheless, when her shift ended the next day, she headed to her compact, two-room home, got into a black dress that was a little more flattering than her uniform, and headed for the Bucket, half expecting to be stood up.

But when she arrived, there he was, waving at her from a table in the corner. She stopped by the bar for her usual whiskey sour from Phineas Gage, which he gave to her on the house, and then she went to join Andy.

"I'm a little surprised you agreed to this, to be honest," Andy said as she took a seat across from him. "I would've thought that, after months of being stuck with me inside a beetle out on Alex, you would've had enough of my company to last a lifetime."

"I must be a sucker for punishment." She offered a grin, to soften the snarkiness.

"Do you ever think about those times?"

Do you? For the first several weeks after returning from their journey, Andy had barely spoken to her. "Sometimes," she said.

"I have to admit, I'm impressed by what you've been able to accomplish since you've gotten back."

Even though Tessa had already told her he'd said that, Lisa was still surprised when she heard it from him. Since returning to Habitat 2, she felt like she'd been grasping for the right choices the entire way, groping in the dark, and only chancing to make anything work. Maybe she was being hard on herself, but that was how it felt, from retaking Habitat 2 to starting her citizen militia. "Well, thanks, Andy. It means a lot, really. Stuff like this, trying to make a difference—it's the reason I came to the inner system from the Belt in the first place."

"Do you miss it? The Belt?"

"I miss my father. My mother died when I was young. Father had to play the role of both parents, and I have to say, he did it well."

"What's he like?"

Lisa paused as she searched for the right words to describe her father, which was something she hadn't had occasion to do very much. People normally didn't ask about her family, or about anything else, really. *Why would they?* She was just a lowly seaman, on the bottom rung of the Darkstream corporate ladder.

"He's kind," she said. "Wise. Deeply distrustful of governments, too, which is the reason he gives for being happier here in the Steele System than he ever was back in the Milky Way. He was always super suspicious of Darkstream, though, too, which got on my nerves sometimes. It was always my dream to work for this company. Not everyone gets to do that, anymore. It's not like it was before."

Andy watched her as she spoke, not attempting to interject with his own opinions, which was good, because they would be irrelevant. He'd never met her father, and likely never would, so what did it matter what he thought about him?

"I say I came out here to make a difference," Lisa went on, "and I did – at least, that's what I tell myself. But others would probably just call it plain old ambition. My father would've said that that's not such a bad thing. He would've called it a good thing, actually. He always said that if I can get to the point where what's best for the world is also best for me, then I'll know I'm on the right path."

"I like that."

"Yeah. Me too. What about you? You're from Eresos, right? Do you miss it there?"

He shook his head. "I had two parents there—have, I guess—but they amounted to less than one, between them. They took no interest in my life. Had no time for me. I was always convinced I was an accident, and one night, when he was drunk, my father admitted it's true: that I was an accident."

"Wow," Lisa said. "I'm sorry, Andy. Though it sort of explains why you have such commitment issues. You're too afraid of getting hurt to let anyone get close."

That brought an extended silence from Andy, and he ran a hand over his freckled chin. She knew she shouldn't have said it, but he *had* hurt her, both after returning from their journey and well before they'd ever left. She wanted him to know that. To acknowledge it, in some way.

"Yeah," he said. "I guess it kind of does." He took a long pull from his beer, which looked to be a stout of some kind. "I don't mean to change the subject, but did you hear that Darkstream released David Lannon and sent him in a shuttle to Valhalla?"

David Lannon was the former head of security for Habitat 2. The one who'd been caught helping Daybreak to enslave the people Lannon had been in charge of protecting.

"To stand trial?"

"No. To evade consequences altogether, it would seem. They're finding him another posting."

"Are you kidding me? That's ridiculous."

Andy shrugged, his shaggy brown hair bouncing a little. "Laudano assured me the move is strictly business. According to him, if Darkstream started prosecuting their employees all over the place—his words, not mine—then they'd receive fewer applications from qualified candidates."

"So they're just sending him elsewhere. To empower criminals to abuse some other innocent people, maybe."

"Maybe."

Lisa shook her head. *I really don't want to have to admit to Tessa that she's right.*

CHAPTER 20

Alliance

The Quatro—he now knew that was what he was, or at least what the humans called his species—soon tired of the chase.

If they'd been able to finish off the human mech, that would've been good, but it wasn't his priority. They had limited time.

He halted, the powerful suit he wore immediately arresting his momentum, and he shouted, "Stop!" The suit's voice boomed through the forest, and the mercenaries that Wound could see came to a halt, turning to study him wearing expressions ranging from wonder to shock.

"Let us return," Wound bellowed, and he began to lope back toward the settlement that he and the human had mostly destroyed with their combat.

Wound was the name he had chosen for himself, after learning from the suit's translation function about the importance of having a name when communicating with humans. The name referenced his blown-off ear, but it also represented something much deeper.

The suit's translator is one of its most powerful weapons. Possibly, it was the most powerful. At least, that was what Wound hoped.

Even so, the suit was a technological and military marvel by any measure. Its versatility seemed almost unlimited, and one of the main limits that did exist was Wound's own imagination.

The suit was capable of morphing to form nearly any weapon he cared to wield, and given enough time, it could manufacture ordnance within itself in preparation for a coming engagement, using materials harvested from Gatherers. It could blast enemies with energy, too, the capacity for which also took some time to recharge.

Most importantly, whoever had built the suit had designed it to detect and amplify the Quatro superconducting ability. It responded to his magnetic nudges by translating them into powerful movements, completely negating the disadvantage Quatro normally experienced aboveground, and instead turning it into an incredible advantage.

The only thing that worried him were the whispers that he'd begun to hear during the quiet moments.

"You are not the humans who attempted to eradicate us from this planet," Wound said to the mercenaries once they were gathered before him inside the circle of wrecked structures. "You are not the ones who filled our tunnels with fire so that our young could not breathe. Instead, you gave us the weapons we needed to oppose the ones who did that. And you just now aided me in battle against one of the indiscriminate killers of your species." Wound swung his head so that he took in all the bipeds standing before him. "Why?"

A man who was large for a human stepped forward. His face was broad and red, as though it endured prolonged exposure to the sun on a regular basis. He spread his hands. "We figured, if we could make friends with great big fellas like you, together we could do a lot more damage to Darkstream than we could've otherwise. I'm Saul, by the way."

"I am Wound. What is Darkstream?"

"They're the ones responsible for all your hardship. I'm a lieutenant in Red Company—we're the good guys. Let me ask you a question. How is it you're able to talk to us right now?"

Wound regarded the man Saul carefully. "It is not I who speaks. It is the suit that I wear. Whoever designed it included the capacity to translate speech from my language to yours. Which I take to mean the designers wished for you and I to converse."

"That thing looks something like the Gatherers and the Amblers. Strange, that they'd leave these machines lying around that end up helping both our species. How did you end up on this planet, anyway, Quatro? I've been hearing word that your species is on Alex, as well."

Wound tilted his head. "Alex?"

That brought a nod from Saul. "It's just what we call the other planet in this system that humanity has business on."

A thrill of excitement ran through Wound's body. "Other Quatro survive in the system? Have they been cast as low as my drift, with all their tools stripped away from them?"

"Well, I don't know what you consider tools, but one of the images I saw showed one of your kind wearing an advanced-looking pressure suit that had two honking big energy weapons attached to it. Back to my question, though, Wound. How'd you end up here?"

"We fled. Back in the Quatro Home System, all are expected to carry out the will of the Assembly of Elders. The Assembly provides all Quatro with the necessities of life, ensuring that all have proper food, shelter, comfort-enabling technologies, as well as machines that safeguard our health. In return, the Assembly expects its beneficiaries to behave exactly as the Assembly wants. The drift that fled to this system, to which I belong—we did not agree that we should be ruled by the dictates of the Assembly just because they provided the basics of life. We viewed those basics as our natural due, and we think that in a just society, the only expected recompense would be to contribute our views toward the governing of that society, while retaining a vast measure of freedom."

As Wound spoke, Saul had nodded along. "It sounds like you Quatro have reasons a lot like ours for coming to this system. It's strange we don't get along better. Hell, from the sounds of it, we should. Why don't we start today? You obviously came to us for a reason. What are you here to propose?"

"The humans have seven more suits just like the one I'm wearing. I do not believe they built them. They had no reason to. I believe they found them, and I believe the discovery has worried them greatly. With the suits in our possession, our chances of defeating this Darkstream will be multiplied by orders of magnitude."

"And you want us to help you secure the suits," Saul said, pointing all five fingers of his left hand at Wound. "Am I right in thinking that?"

"Yes."

"What's in it for us?"

"Once we kill the murderers of Darkstream, you may have the suits they wield."

Saul was nodding again. "Boy, do I love the sound of that."

Something whispered to Wound from within the suit, then, and he snapped his head sideways, which made some of the mercenaries jump.

That was the loudest one yet.

But he still hadn't been able to make out the words.

CHAPTER 21

Infiltration

L isa paused before crossing the corridor, inching her assault rifle around the corner and sticking her head out momentarily to check for enemies.

Clear.

She dashed on, alert for the sound of gunfire, ready to execute a tactical roll at a moment's notice if the need for evasive maneuvers arose.

"Seaman Apprentice Miller, what's your status?" she asked over the squad-wide channel.

"Some Daybreak goons have us pinned in one of their laboratories, but they seem hesitant to cause too much damage to it. We're using that to our advantage."

"Good work," Lisa said, just as she heard something skittering across the floor of the facility. Looking down, she saw it was a flashbang.

Kicking it away as fast as she could, she leapt toward a nearby hatch, with the intention of opening it and seeking cover there. But when she slapped the control panel, it refused to open.

The flashbang went off, but Lisa had closed her eyes, mitigating the effects somewhat, though it did cause her ears to ring shrilly.

She dove again, just as a burst of rifle fire scored the closed hatch. Rolling onto her back, Lisa spotted her adversary and leveled her SL-17 at her. She fired.

The white-haired woman also jumped out of the way in time, taking refuge behind the corner Lisa had just turned. Tessa Notaras was just as fast as the stories about her claimed, it seemed. She was arguably Quentin Cooper's best operative, and she was known for her ruthlessness.

Regaining her feet as quietly as she could, Lisa crept down the corridor toward Tessa's cover, doing everything she could to make no sound. She doubted her adversary would expect the move, and when she popped out to fire again, Lisa hoped to take her unawares.

But instead of Tessa's face or torso, a grenade came around the corner. Lisa turned to flee, but it was too late. The grenade exploded directly underneath her, blowing her apart.

The simulation deposited her back into the high-lucidity lobby, where most of the participants were already waiting, including Andy.

"Things didn't go so well in the labs?" Lisa asked.

"Nah," Andy said, shaking his head. "I guess they cared less about the equipment than I thought. Looks like Daybreak wins this one, judging by who's here already." Phineas Gage, Bob O'Toole, and several others from the team tasked with infiltrating the Daybreak hillside facility were also in the lobby, meaning they'd died in the sim. "Who got you?" Andy asked.

"Tessa. It was close, though. Sort of."

This was the umpteenth time Lisa had gotten her militia to run this scenario, and she would likely get them to do it umpteen times more. For one thing, it helped them to better grasp the principles of a good defense, when they were on the side of the Daybreak defenders. For another, it gave them practice performing a strike with the aim of disabling a facility, which was exactly what Lisa planned to do to Daybreak in real life, after successfully defending Habitat 2 from them.

As an added bonus, the exercise would hopefully help them get inside the heads of Daybreak's operatives a little more.

The objective of the scenario was for the invaders to reach the facility's life support system and blow it up. That had happened in roughly three-fifths of the simulations, which Lisa viewed as a promising sign. That said, there was a very strong correlation between the winning team and whatever side Tessa Notaras happened to be on.

Soon, the simulation ended, with Daybreak having successfully defended their illegal settlement. Now, everyone waited in the high-lucidity lobby while Lisa set up the next scenario.

"We're running the same one again," Lisa said. "This time, we're switching sides."

Without any more warning than that, she loaded them all into the simulation again.

Lisa's team fared a little better in this one, despite Tessa still being on the opposing side. The older woman had been teaching

Lisa about commanding a unit—tactics, formations, prioritizing objectives, and so on. Unfortunately, that made it fairly easy for Tessa to recognize whatever approach her pupil was trying.

Even so, Lisa felt proud when they succeeded in holding out against Tessa's onslaught for the longest period yet. Tessa herself even went down, to a lucky shot from Andy. But in the end, the opposing team pressed on toward the life support infrastructure, and victory.

Lisa managed to survive for the entire simulation, this time, which she decided to view as a minor victory, as well.

In the seconds before the simulation ended, it always gave her a few moments of increased lucidity, during which she became aware again that she was not in fact a member of Daybreak trying to protect their secret facility.

This time, during those brief moments before getting sent back to the lobby, she strolled around a bit, wondering how accurately their implants had depicted the hillside facility. They knew it existed, based on the intel she'd extracted from Leonardo Fiore, but they knew nothing about its layout.

A figure appeared at the end of the corridor she walked along. Lisa didn't recognize him as a member of her militia, and his behavior wasn't typical of the simulation's AI.

When he saw her, he turned to run.

Lisa brought her assault rifle up, spraying the corridor with bullets in a line, meaning to cut across the man's legs. She was trying to disable him, so she could catch up and identify him before the simulation ended.

But then it did end, and she was back in the lobby with the others. The man she'd seen was not among them.

"You look spooked, Lisa," Andy said. "Did you see something?"

"I saw someone who shouldn't be there."

"Who?"

"Not sure. I'm guessing it was either a Darkstream employee or a Daybreak operative...unless it was someone else altogether. Either way, none of those options seem great."

CHAPTER 22

Imminent Danger

Jake and Ash walked the perimeter of the camp, outside of their mechs, assault rifles held at the ready, pistols in holsters, and a healthy helping of grenades distributed among their persons. Plus, a couple of combat knives each.

They were trying to follow Roach's command to spend as much time as possible out of their mechs—during the night watches, in the evenings before sleep, and in the mornings before they started out for the day.

"Still can't believe the chief put you in charge and not me," Ash said, her short, light-blond hair waving as she walked. "I'm clearly smarter and more resourceful than you."

Jake laughed. "I'm not about to disagree with that, Steam. But the smartest people don't always make the best leaders. I think Chief Roach recognizes that."

"What? That doesn't make any sense. Of course they make the best leaders. They're smart."

"I don't mean your ability to lead is less because you're smarter. You'd probably make a better leader than me, in a lot of ways. But that doesn't mean much if your subordinates won't follow orders as readily as they follow mine."

"Why wouldn't they?"

"Because I'm dumber than you. And people trust dumb people way more than they trust smart ones."

Ash paused, seeming to contemplate the idea. "You know, that does ring kind of true."

They walked on. Somewhere on the other side of the camp, Beth and Richaud would be doing the same thing. The night remained quiet, just as every night had since the attack when the Quatro had liberated one of the quads. Oneiri Team took turns with the Force Multipliers and the soldiers from the Plenitos garrison in patrolling the camp at night, though Oneiri took a disproportionate number of shifts.

Jake had requested that, to build time outside the mechs into their journey. For their part, the soldiers from the other divisions didn't seem to have much problem with taking fewer watches.

No one's about to turn down extra sleep.

"Do you think the chief will make it back?" Ash said as they rounded one of the armored personnel carriers.

"Well, he's made it through a lot."

"He has, but I'm worried about his mental state, lately."

"You too, eh?"

"We all are," Ash said.

"Really? I was making a point not to bring it up to the team. I didn't want to bring morale down any lower than it is."

"Well, we're not stupid. Anyone can see Chief Roach is falling apart. Part of me wants to say you should have tried to prevent him from chasing the quad. But I doubt I would've had the guts to do anything different, in your position."

Jake decided to change the subject. "Have you heard from your mother, lately?"

Ash nodded. "Yeah. She's settling into Valhalla."

"Wow. Valhalla, eh?"

"Yep. My father left a fair number of credits behind when he died, and she's too scared to stay on Eresos, considering the Quatro managed to get inside Plenitos and the same thing nearly happened to Ingress."

"I can hardly blame her. I'd get out of here in her position, too, if I had the credits. Or if I didn't have access to a giant robot to protect me."

A chuckle from Ash. "How about you? Have you been getting any messages from your family?"

"Yeah," Jake said with a long sigh. "I have. Sue Anne took a turn for the worse, last week. The doctors aren't giving her very much longer."

"Oh, wow. I'm so sorry to hear that, Jake."

"Thanks. It's weird, you know. Sue Anne's been such a large part of my life, for so many years, and yet I barely feel like I know her. I mean, sure, we lived together for the first five years of her life, but then she got sick, and soon after that me and dad started up the comet development business to try to raise enough money for her treatment." Jake shook his head. "Sue Anne's why I'm on Oneiri Team at all. I mean, yes, it's my dream, but thinking of how much the pay would do for her got me through training, and it keeps me acting like an okay soldier and not questioning orders too much. It gives me my drive in battle. If she goes..."

"You're going to be okay, Jake. No matter what happens, you're going to be okay. You have us. You have your team. And we have you. We need you, as a matter of fact."

"Thanks, Ash."

Beth's voice came over the team-wide channel. "Clutch. Steam. We have something over here."

"What is it?" Jake said.

"Richaud thinks he just saw a man running off through the trees. Looks like he might have been spying on the camp. You think it was someone from Red Company?"

"Possibly." At least it wasn't a Quatro. Red Company, they could deal with fairly easily, or so Jake figured. He pondered whether he should wake the rest of Oneiri Team and order them into their mechs, until they were certain no danger was imminent. "If you see anything else, anything at all that seems out of place or unusual, let me know straight away."

"Will do."

"Jake!"

He turned, and immediately, he saw what had put so much fear into Ash's voice.

It was the stolen quad, barreling toward them at full gallop.

CHAPTER 23

Back in Business

Both Jake and Ash turned as one, barreling back through the camp. As they did, Force Multiplier and Plenitos soldiers closed around them, doing whatever they could to try to slow the charging quad.

And just as fast as they lined up to oppose it, they died.

Ash reached her mech first, and Jake saw her pop a sedative into her mouth before slapping the machine's calf and climbing up the ramp that lowered.

He breathed a sigh of relief that she'd made it to safety. But he didn't dare stop to celebrate.

Instead, he asked everything of his body that it had to give as he strove toward his own mech, which was several meters away.

Fumbling with the belt pouch that held his fast-acting sedatives, he finally got one out and into his mouth. Rounding his MIMAS' leg, Jake slammed his palm into the biometric sensor on the back of it. The ramp lowered promptly, and he clambered inside his mech, already beginning to feel better—safer.

He started to slip into lucid, but before the ramp had time to close, the quad crashed into the front of the **MIMAS**, knocking it backward so that it slammed against the ground.

Jake was half-asleep, his body partially drooping out of his mech. With a great effort, he pulled himself back into the cockpit, grunting, pain making his body spasm.

At last, he managed it, and the back of the **MIMAS** sealed up.

Back in business, he thought from within lucid, ignoring the med-alerts telling him he'd pulled at least two muscles while straining against gravity.

Turning on the spot, he scanned his surroundings for the quad, but it had moved on to another foe—or, more accurately, *foes.* The thing rampaged through the camp, cutting through the ranks of humans like a scythe through wheat.

Jake would have pursued, but he had his own foes to deal with. The camp wasn't just under attack by the quad—there were also Quatro all around them, fighting to access the personnel carriers, and humans as well.

Red Company. That seemed certain, now.

Jake fired up his flamethrowers, using the streams of flame to sweep several targets at once.

A Red Company fighter ran toward him, grenades clutched in both hands, and Jake simply raised his foot, stomping the human so that he slammed backward onto the hard ground.

Stepping forward, Jake's left foot found the man's head, causing it to pop like an overripe melon. He didn't even turn when the twin explosions ripped through the night.

Stowing the flamethrowers for now, he forewent his rotary autocannons as well, wary of hitting friendlies with their powerful yet somewhat less controlled spray of armor-piercing rounds.

Instead, he detached the heavy machine gun from his back and chose his targets carefully.

A Quatro went down to a prolonged burst. Then he lined up the machine gun with a row of three humans, who were creeping toward a personnel carrier, clearly trying to be stealthy. Jake put bullets in their backs, and they all went down, never to rise again.

When he realized that everyone surrounding him were enemies, he switched to his autocannons after all, mowing down as many foes as he could.

It wasn't enough. The combined numbers of Quatro and Red Company were overwhelming the remnants of the Force Multipliers, and the Plenitos garrison soldiers weren't used to this sort of pitched combat.

Backed up by the evident power of the quad, the enemy seemed unstoppable. The Darkstream battalion was crumpling, and not even the combined might of Oneiri Team could stop it.

The Quatro had almost reached the personnel carriers, where they clearly planned to enter quads of their own. If that happened, Jake was certain the night would be lost altogether.

"*Jake.*" It was Chief Roach's voice, coming over what Jake's HUD told him was a two-way channel.

Hearing his first name in Roach's voice gave him a momentary sense of surreality as he continued to unload with his autocannons. "Uh...sir?"

"Turn around."

Jake did, stopping the stream of bullets and stowing the autocannons by reforming his mech's hands in front of them.

He saw Gabe's mech walking out of the woods toward him, but it was moving oddly—stumbling, limbs moving in a fashion that was awkward and cumbersome. Certainly not how they'd been designed to move.

The mech itself had a *crumpled* look, with dents and deep furrows all over it, as well as a massive scorch mark all down its right side.

"I see you did a fine job with taking command," Roach said, his voice acidic. With that, the chief switched to a team-wide channel. "Oneiri Team, this is Chief Roach. You are to abandon this camp and rendezvous at a location I will send your implants. *Now.*"

"But, sir..." Ash said. "The quads! And Tommy's mech!"

"Listen to me, Sweeney. If we stay, we will be defeated by the Quatro, who will soon access those quads. There's no preventing that. The camp is lost, and if we remain, the mercenaries will kill us and get our mechs, too."

"What about the Force Multipliers?" Jake said. "And the soldiers from Plenitos?"

"They're *lost,*" Roach barked. "And so will all of Eresos be if you don't do your job and follow my order, right now."

CHAPTER 24

On Patrol

Lisa missed having Rug and Tessa with her during patrols of the city streets. Returning to her old duties was a change in more ways than one, and few of them were exactly pleasant.

Other than the lack of companionship, and her diminished role and authority, she also felt fairly tired most of the time.

She attributed that to the training she conducted every night with her militia. Even though they did it while sleeping, there was no question that lucid affected quality of sleep.

She refused to take stims except during battle, and even then only when she truly needed them. Coffee, on the other hand, she drank by the gallon.

It's worth it. To hold on to Habitat 2, it's all *worth it.*

Today, her patrolling mattered more than it normally did. The entire Darkstream battalion had donned pressure suits and headed outside Habitat 2, to scout the surrounding terrain at the request of the council, so that they could prepare for the coming battle with Daybreak.

The idea was to consider each possible attack angle, and also what the defensive strategy would be for each one.

Lisa would not be a part of those discussions. Even though she'd played a major role in retaking Habitat 2 from Daybreak, she was still just a lowly seaman as far as Darkstream was concerned.

Before the Darkstream soldiers fanned out of Habitat 2 to scout the neighborhood, Lisa had covertly contacted Rug over an encrypted channel, warning her and the other Quatro not to remain near the city for the time being. A chance encounter between Darkstream and Rug's drift was the last thing they needed. Not to mention the last thing *Lisa* needed.

A man farther down the street caught her eye, and she started walking briskly toward him. He seemed to notice her approach, slipping into an alley as though to hide from her.

I'm sure that was Samuel Dalton. He was the Daybreak member who she'd offered leniency to, in exchange for information on Quentin Cooper.

Except, he was supposed to be in a jail cell.

She quickly checked her SL-17's action and broke into a run. Her first impulse was to barrel around the corner and into the alley, but remembering her training from Tessa, she checked that impulse.

Her restraint saved her life. Two more soldiers waited with Dalton in the alley, and all of them were armed.

As soon as her head appeared around the corner, all three of them pointed their guns at her. She pulled back just as they began to fire.

Lisa wasn't authorized to carry actual grenades while on patrol, because of the risk of structural damage to Habitat 2.

Luckily, she *was* authorized to carry flashbangs, and she had one on her today. She ripped it from her belt, activated it, cooked it for a second, and tossed it into the alleyway.

It worked exactly as advertised, disorienting the trio of escaped prisoners with a deafening *bang* and a flash of bright light.

Lisa huddled against the structure she was using for cover as it went off, plugging her ears, and then she walked backward into the street until her first target came into view.

It was Dalton, and he had his hands clamped to his ears. She shot him in the chest, and he dropped.

That's one of the major disadvantages of being an escaped prisoner. No body armor.

Moving to the left, she got the next Daybreak operative, a woman, in the throat.

The third fired wildly out of the alley, but none of her shots hit, and Lisa put her down as well.

That done, she switched on a channel she'd set up weeks ago but had yet to use—one that gave her direct access to every member of her militia.

"The Daybreak prisoners have escaped," she subvocalized. "I just took down three of them, but if they released their friends as well, and I don't know why they wouldn't have, then we have dozens more to contend with. I'm transmitting my location to your implants. Make your way toward me, but proceed with extreme caution, and unite with each other along the way whenever you can. Sato out."

I wonder where the prisoners got their guns. Not that firearms were hard to acquire inside Habitat 2.

She began running along the street she'd been patrolling, toward the jail where the prisoners had been kept. It was fairly close to here, meaning the other Daybreak operatives were likely to be near.

The thought that Daybreak might retake Habitat 2 while most of her Darkstream colleagues were out on Alex, without Quentin Cooper even needing to show up—well, she just couldn't let that happen.

CHAPTER 25

Constable Station

Out of necessity, every structure in Habitat 2 was the same height: two stories. The ceiling—comprised of parallelogram lights designed to simulate skylight with the sun beaming through—capped buildings at that level, and if you reached up with a broom from a second-floor balcony, you'd hit it with the bristles.

It was the balconies that now gave Lisa the most trouble: few buildings had them, but there were enough to make defending against three dimensions a real thing.

A prisoner popped above one now, firing down on her with a shotgun.

Lisa reacted instantly, diving behind a hoverbike nearby and making sure to position herself behind the engine block, which was the only part of hoverbikes that offered real protection from gunfire.

When the shooting stopped, she popped up immediately, hitting the balcony with suppressive fire while walking backward toward a nearby alley.

She stopped shooting, as though she needed to reload, at which time she would have typically taken cover.

But she didn't actually need to reload, and when the Daybreak fighter appeared above the balcony again, she put the two rounds left in her clip right in his face.

I'm getting tired of this.

A soft, high-pitched whine came from behind her, which she recognized as the sound of an approaching hoverbike. She swung around while slamming another clip into place at the same time.

It was Andy, applying steady power to his forward propulsor so that he came to a stop directly beside her.

"Need a lift?" he said.

"Thought you'd never ask." She climbed onto the bike behind Andy and wrapped her left arm around him while letting her right dangle, assault rifle nestled against the hoverbike's side.

Andy gunned the motor, and they continued in the direction Lisa had been headed.

"Seems they're headed toward the Darkstream Constable Station," he subvocalized.

"Yeah. Not really surprising. That's where they'll have access to the airlock overrides. Where they can prevent the Darkstream soldiers from getting back into Habitat 2."

Andy chuckled, which sounded flat, subvocalized as it was. "I have to wonder how they knew to time this so well."

"I have to wonder how they escaped in the first place."

"Let's wonder later. Looks like we have company."

Andy patched his view of the street ahead through to Lisa's implant. It showed three Daybreak goons running to take cover from them.

"Ready?" Andy subvocalized.

"Ready," Lisa answered, not exactly sure what he was planning, though she had an idea.

He engaged the forward propulsor while easing up on the back one, causing them to swing around until they were coming at the Daybreak goons sideways.

Lisa raised her gun, catching one of them out in the open, dropping her, and clipping another one in the arm before he managed to conceal himself.

Then, Andy was accelerating into a side alley.

"I wonder if they know Habitat 2 as well as I do," Andy subvocalized. "Doubt it. No one's cruised these streets more than me."

"What's the upshot, Andy?" Lisa said, not quite in the mood for his boasting at the moment.

"This alley connects with the one they're taking cover next to. Ready to get high?"

"Punch it."

Andy cut through the network of alleyways, handling each corner like a champ. Soon, they were headed in the opposite direction—straight at the pair of remaining Daybreak fighters.

As Andy sped up, Lisa remembered him saying that he'd modified his hoverbike so that it was capable of exceeding the speed cap Darkstream installed to prevent accidents within the confines of Habitat 2.

As he accelerated, the hoverbike went higher, until Lisa worried they would collide with the artificial ceiling.

They sailed over the heads of their foes, who were gaping upward, slowly raising their guns to track them.

Too late.

Lisa fired off one round, two. Both escaped convicts hit the ground.

"That was fun," she subvocalized. "Let's do it again."

"Yes, ma'am."

Bob O'Toole's voice came over the militia-wide channel. "Lisa, I mean ma'am, me and Rodney Vickers and a few others are holding out against a more than two dozen Daybreak asshats, here in front of the Constable Station. We're giving them everything we got, but there's a lot of them, and I'm scared they're gonna break through our defense soon."

"Acknowledged, O'Toole," Lisa said. "Tessa, you hearing this?"

"Sure am. Meet you there?"

"You got it. Just tell me when you're in position."

When Lisa and Andy arrived, thirty Daybreak fighters had O'Toole and the others pinned inside the Darkstream Constable Station. The enemy fighters were crouched behind hoverbikes of their own, which they must have stolen along the way.

"Tessa? How are you looking?"

"Peachy. You?"

"We're here. Hit them now."

Andy veered into the square in front of the Constable Station, executing a controlled fishtail so that Lisa could hit the enemy formation from behind.

Several of them turned to fire back, and Andy came to a stop.

"Take cover behind the engine block, Andy," Lisa shouted. "The *engine block.* And cover me!"

For her part, Lisa leapt off the hoverbike, running across the square while firing at the nearest enemy fighters, who shot back at her.

Andy's covering fire kept some of the pressure off of Lisa. Then, directly above the Daybreak fighters, the ceiling broke apart as four parallelogram lights shifted aside.

Tessa and the four-person team she'd led across Habitat 2's roof rappelled down, still wearing pressure suits. They came to a halt in midair and fired on Daybreak from above.

Lisa reached the alley she'd been making for, using the combination of adequate cover and the enemy's disorientation to open fire.

The soldiers suspended in the air rained bullets onto the enemy's head, and emboldened, O'Toole and those with him emerged from the Darkstream Constable Station, guns blazing.

The escaped prisoners threw down their guns and put their hands in the air.

"We surrender. We surrender, you bastards!"

Of the original thirty soldiers, there were eleven left.

"We accept," Lisa said. "I just hope you've learned your lesson. Now get back in your cells."

CHAPTER 26

If I Bleed, I Bleed

'm slowing them down.

On his way back to Oneiri Team, Gabe had been sure the mercenaries and the quad were about to catch and kill him at any minute.

His mech was badly damaged, the servomotors failing and the actuators misaligned.

To return, he'd essentially needed to learn to walk again, on the fly. He'd quickly figured out that when he tried to walk forward, he listed dramatically to the left, but the stutter in his right leg was random, impossible to predict, and he tripped several times. His left arm was almost totally useless, but the right still mostly worked.

"I'm slowing you down," he said to the rest of Oneiri Team. *Did I say that already?* "You need to go on. Save your mechs. Mine will probably be useless to the enemy, anyway. I doubt they'll be able to repair it."

"*No,* sir," Jake Price said.

"Excuse me, Seaman Apprentice?" Gabe stopped walking to glare at Price.

"I said no. I refuse to follow that order. We aren't abandoning you to the enemy. I'm prepared to declare you unfit for command, if that's what it takes to disobey that command and get you to safety. Failing that, I'm ready to be straight-up insubordinate. But we're all getting out of this alive. *All* of us. We're not leaving anybody behind."

Gabe stared at Price, feeling wretched, his mech curled in on itself even as he stood still. "*Fine,*" he spat.

Price only nodded, and they continued on, the others marching and Gabe limping, his feet dragging across the ground.

He forced the mech to increase its pace, in an awkward, stumbling run that he felt sure was difficult to behold. But they needed to speed up. Otherwise, they were all done.

There'll be harsh discipline for Price if we get out of this. He's endangering all of Eresos by risking the MIMAS mechs.

But Gabe doubted he would survive long enough to administer that discipline.

"Sir..." Ash Sweeney said.

"What, Steam?"

"Your vitals, sir. I just had a look at them. You're bleeding out."

"It's irrelevant," he said.

"You have several broken bones. Your suit has detected internal bleeding. I have to insist that we stop now so we can give you first aid."

"No *way* are we stopping," Gabe said, his voice strained. "If we stop long enough for me to fall out of my mech, so you can take turns playing nurse with me, then we'll *all* need medical attention. The Quatro are close behind us, I can guarantee you that."

Price stepped forward. "Sir," he said, clearly trying to sound authoritative.

Gabe raised his one functioning arm, his hand splitting apart to expose the rotary autocannon waiting behind it. "Yes, Price? What is it you need me to do in order for you to get it through your air-filled head how serious I am?" The autocannon began to spin.

"All right, sir," Price said quietly. "All right."

They pressed on.

As they did, Gabe said, "The mercenaries already have Tommy's mech, and I expect they'll figure out how to override the biometric lock in short order. If they left those tanks intact, then they have those, too. If I bleed out, I bleed out, and if that happens, you are to destroy my mech beyond all use or recognition. I will *not* empower our enemies just because you're all acting like a bunch of bleeding hearts."

CHAPTER 27

A Lot to Answer For

After they finished re-incarcerating the Daybreak prisoners, Lisa and Tessa went back on patrol, just like old times, as they waited for the Darkstream soldiers to return.

Other than Daybreak members and soldiers of Lisa's militia, there were only two casualties among the habitat's civilian population, both injuries from which the victims were expected to make full recoveries.

One of Lisa's soldiers had died, and two more had suffered fairly serious injuries. Those incidents were tragic, but Lisa considered the civilian casualties totally unacceptable.

She knew it could have been a lot worse. Still, the prisoners should never have gotten free in the first place.

"We need to find out how they escaped," Lisa muttered.

Tessa turned to her as they walked, her expression grim. "Yes. We do. But I don't think you're going to like the answer, once we find it."

To that, Lisa had nothing to say. She kept her eyes on the surrounding buildings. Very little structural damage had been done during the attack, so they'd been fairly lucky, there.

"I didn't see the Darkstream operatives surveying *anything* while my team and I were getting into position on the roof," Tessa said. "I didn't see them at all, as a matter of fact. It was almost as if they cleared out intentionally, so that they couldn't possibly come to our aid when the Daybreak prisoners broke out."

Once, Lisa would have immediately condemned Tessa's comments as needless conspiracy theorizing. Now, she found herself without any words for them.

Then, unexpectedly, she found some: "Habitat 2 is big," she said. "The Darkstream soldiers might have been out of your line of sight." But even she could hear how halfhearted that sounded.

Tessa shook her head. "You need to start putting together the pieces, g..."

Glancing at her sharply, Lisa said, "You almost called me girl again."

Tessa's mouth formed a thin line. "Look at what's happened to us, since Daybreak took over the first time. Darkstream's attempts to reclaim Habitat 2 were basically nonexistent. Out on Alex, we had our system net access blocked, in a way that could only happen if someone powerful was directly targeting us. And now this. I appreciate how loyal you are. I think it's one of your best traits—I really do. But it's begun to verge on insanity. You need to wake up."

Lisa shook her head. Everything she'd dreamed of, everything she'd worked toward... everything she'd always believed Darkstream stood for.

Profits, yes, of course—but also security. Everyone in the Steele System benefited from the stable environment the company created. And those that worked hard, who were smart, who acquired enough money because of the genuine contributions to society that they'd made...well, they could afford even more security. They could afford to hire Darkstream military operatives, to protect them from the danger that lurked everywhere.

Everywhere in the universe, it seems.

Tessa was calling all of that into question. She was attacking the idea that Darkstream was the force keeping a lid on evil—indeed, she was arguing that Darkstream itself was a *source* of evil.

It had Lisa's stomach in knots as she tried to contend with the idea. Bile crept up her throat, and she forced it down, only for it to surge back up again.

"Lisa?" Tessa said. "Are you okay?"

What would my father say? She took a moment to cast her fevered mind back to the Belt, where her father toiled. Part of her believed that he would always be there, toiling eternally, and that she'd be able to visit him any time.

He would have agreed with Tessa. Without a doubt. Her father had never trusted Darkstream.

"Seaman Sato," a voice said, coming through her implant. It was Commander Laudano.

"Yes, sir?" she said. "Have you and the others returned? I have a lot to report."

"I'd say you do. A lot to answer for, too. Get to my office in the Darkstream Constable Station, right now."

CHAPTER 28

Contract Violation

"Close the door," Laudano said once she entered his office, his voice steel.

She complied, turning to come to attention and salute.

He took a seat behind his desk, but did not offer for her to sit in one of the three chairs reserved for visitors.

"Would you like to tell me about what happened while I was away?"

"Certainly, sir. The Daybreak prisoners escaped their cells. We haven't been able to ascertain how, yet—as far as we can tell, they somehow accessed the keycards to open them. We managed to stop their incursion. That required killing most of them, but the remaining prisoners are back in jail."

"You keep saying *we*," Laudano said, his eyes never leaving hers. "What do you mean by *we?*"

Lisa cleared her throat. "Uh, I had the help of some of the other residents of Habitat 2."

"Yes, clearly, but there was something different about these residents, was there not? They seemed to have a reasonably high level of training in firearms, as well as unit tactics in an urban environment. The sort of training that only a member of a professional military body could have imparted. Do you have any idea how these *residents* came to benefit from such training, seaman?"

Lisa's eyes found the floor. "I trained them, sir."

"Of course you did. I knew that already; I just needed to get your confession on record. Are you aware of the consequences of insubordination, Seaman Sato?"

Whatever you want them to be? "Yes, sir," she said.

"I am well within my rights to discharge you dishonorably—and that's just for insubordination. For violating your contract with Darkstream, which also forbids passing on the training we have given you to others, the company can sue you into oblivion. Either way, your name would be disgraced throughout the Steele System, and your aged father would hang his head in shame, I am sure of that. I told you not to give these residents the gift of military training. By doing so, you have granted them a dangerous weapon, without the sense of duty and honor that is meant to accompany it."

But I have emphasized the importance of duty and honor. And most of them didn't need to be told in the first place.

It was an argument that Lisa could hold only in her head, however. She was already in deep enough trouble without contradicting Laudano more than she already had.

"I'm prepared to accept whatever consequences you deem fit, sir," she said. Though if Laudano actually intended to dishonorably discharge her, she expected he would have done it without all the fanfare.

Laudano wants something else from me.

"Yes, I expect you *are* prepared. But perhaps we can arrive at a situation where there is no need for me to administer any consequences."

Here we go.

"The resource collection from the Gatherers," Laudano went on, "though it took a sharp dip before and during the battle you fought to retake Habitat 2, has gone way up since then. I've been monitoring the reports closely, and it wasn't a momentary spike caused by a glitch in the machines. No, this is sustained. Do you know why that might be, Seaman?"

Lisa did know why, and her lip trembled as she struggled with the question of whether she should volunteer the information. No doubt Laudano would extract it anyway, but she didn't want to betray the Quatro by passing on their secret. That said, Rug had never asked her to conceal it from anyone.

"You really need to start being more forthcoming with me, Sato," Laudano said, with a sigh. "Very well. We will walk through it, shall we? To have increased resource collection, you must have increased Gatherer traffic to Habitat 2, meaning you have discovered how to influence the machines somehow. I can only assume your Quatro friends helped you to do so. If you want to escape your dishonorable discharge, you will tell me how this was done. Immediately."

Now, it was Lisa's turn to sigh, much more tremulously than Laudano had. "You have to feed them a very particular amount of a resource they aren't currently collecting. I don't know the amounts, but I do know they correspond to deposits scattered throughout the planet. If you feed one just the right amount of terbium, for example, it'll start harvesting from the corresponding terbium deposit."

A smile grew like a cancer across Laudano's face. "Congratulations, Sato. You have escaped discharge this day. You may return to your duties of patrolling the streets of Habitat 2 and never sticking your nose where it doesn't belong, ever again. Further, if you are caught training civilians anymore, you will find yourself not just discharged, but also incarcerated. Do I make myself clear, Sato?"

"Clear, sir."

"Dismissed, then."

CHAPTER 29

Significant Deviations

Since Roach was unable to concentrate on anything other than staggering forward in his battered mech, Jake retained the command, if only in function and not in name.

He ordered Oneiri Team to stick as close behind him as he could, though he regularly glanced back, to make sure Chief Roach was keeping up.

In the meantime, he randomized their path as much as he could, in an attempt to throw off pursuers. That said, it was difficult to conceal the passage of seven MIMAS mechs.

Then they hit the Barrens, and the terrain changed so radically it was as though they'd teleported to another planet.

During their first trip through this region, on their way to help break the Siege of Plenitos, Jake remembered thinking that if he had to come up with a single word to describe the Barrens, it would have been "vertical."

Sheer, craggy cliffs seemed to be their chief characteristic, and his implant had helpfully volunteered the information that the Barrens were known for their frequent volcanic activity; one of the main reasons very few humans lived here.

The Gatherers traversed the Barrens just fine, of course. Nothing seemed to ever impede *their* progress.

Jake's mind kept flashing back to the memory of his fellow Darkstream soldiers back in the camp, fighting for their lives, and falling by the dozen.

We left them. Abandoned them.

They'd been following orders when they'd done it, but that didn't change things. Yes, they'd left to keep the **MIMAS** mechs out of enemy hands. And that was a positive thing, from a strategic perspective.

It still doesn't change the fact that we spent the lives of good men and women to accomplish it.

"Clutch." It was Ash, subvocalizing over a two-way channel.

"Yeah, Steam?" he said, too focused on keeping his footing on the uneven landscape to look back at her.

"The quads..."

That made him look. Far behind them, appearing as tiny specks on the sere landscape, were the Quatro in the mechs they'd stolen.

They were gaining ground rapidly. Even as he watched, the tiny specks grew in size.

"We need to move faster." Jake looked at Roach. "Sir, we have to speed up."

"Easy for you to say," Roach growled. "I told you to leave me behind."

"Sir, we're operating under the same principle we did outside the walls of Plenitos. If you stay behind, we all stay behind, and then we fight the quads together, probably losing in the process. So if you consider it important strategically to keep the MIMAS mechs from the enemy, I suggest you find a way to speed up."

Roach didn't answer. Instead, his mech did speed up, and because he'd left his transponder on, they all could hear the agonized screaming that accompanied the effort.

Jake turned back and continued leading Oneiri Team across the Barrens of Eresos. They bounded across ravines, leapt from hilltop to hilltop, and sprinted across brief stretches of flat terrain as fast as they could.

It didn't seem to make a difference. The quads still gained steadily, and in the meantime, a sheer cliff rose up in front of Oneiri Team.

That thing must be two-hundred feet high.

"You all see that cliff? When we reach it, I want you to jump as high as you can—find a handhold somehow. Use your launch thrusters, if you need to. I can guarantee you that those quads can't climb as well as we can. It's the same principle as hiding from a bear in a tree."

He'd tried to sound confident, but the fact was that they were still in uncharted territory when it came to exploring the MIMAS mechs' capabilities. Yes, they knew what the designers *claimed* they could do, but there'd already been significant deviations between those claims and reality.

Jake had sent an evac request to Bronson well before they'd entered the Barrens. No shuttles had yet been built large enough to accommodate the mechs, and so escaping a planet quickly involved using the mechs' rockets to achieve low orbit, to land on a waiting warship.

Unfortunately, the maneuver required considerable precision, and Bronson wasn't even in position yet. Once he arrived, Oneiri Team would have to execute the launch on the run from the quads.

Speaking of the Quatro...

When he glanced back, he saw that they were hot on Oneiri Team's heels, a mere fifty meters away.

Good God. Their speed was unbelievable. Jake turned to run backwards for a while, risking losing his footing on the treacherous terrain. He flashed back to training on Valhalla, when Roach had frequently demanded they run backwards

Now I know why.

Jake loosed rockets at the quads in front. Great explosions blossomed on the dry terrain, and the quads did make the effort to evade them, which bought Oneiri a few seconds. But no more than that.

He continued to fire rockets at whichever Quatro was in the lead. Once his payload was spent, he said, "Steam, use your remaining rockets to do what I just did, and Arkanian, you do the same after Steam is finished. We need more time."

One by one, Oneiri Team turned to run backward while firing on the chasing quads, allowing the MIMAS mechs to inch closer to the cliff that was their goal.

But their rockets ran out with the cliff still a considerable distance away. And the front quad had almost reached the rear MIMAS.

Jake stopped running. "Keep going!" he barked at the others.

That was all he had time to say. The quad was upon him, and Jake charged straight into it, both bayonets extended.

The alien knocked him backward with a shocking abruptness. One instant he was grappling with the quad; the next he lay flat on his back, pinned by the thing, who looked like it was about to savage him.

A blur of dark-gray and orange streaked toward the alien. It was Ash, using her launch thrusters to tackle the Quatro.

It worked. The quad rolled sideways, scrabbling for purchase on the sunbaked clay. Ash found her footing faster than the alien, arresting her momentum and dashing back toward Jake, extending her hand toward him.

He took it, and she flipped him to his feet. Together, they chased after the rest of Oneiri Team.

"Surely *now* we're even," Ash said.

"Not quite," Jake said.

"Seriously?"

"Yeah. I owe *you*, now."

CHAPTER 30

Jump

The cliff loomed before them, with the Quatro practically nipping at their heels.

Within the dream, the sky yawned open, revealing a widening scarlet chasm. The ground appeared to steam, and periodically the world flashed blood-red.

The mech dream was doing everything it could to make sure Jake knew exactly how much danger he was in.

He didn't really need the reminder. The power of the quad he'd taken on had astounded him, and he was still reeling from getting slammed into the ground. Med-diagnostics flashed in the upper left of his HUD, informing him that he needed the attention of iatric nanobots as soon as possible, to repair some internal bleeding. It was odd to have to be told by the interface that he was hurt, while he felt every injury to the mech itself as though it were his own.

I wonder if iatric nanobots will be enough to return Chief Roach to health.

He'd snuck a glance at Roach's vitals, just as he was sure the rest of Oneiri had. If he was being honest, it seemed amazing that Roach still lived to operate the mech, let alone remain conscious. The chief wouldn't have been able to move at all if it wasn't for the MIMAS carrying him, even if it did run in a bizarre, stuttering fashion.

At last, they drew close enough to the cliff.

"*Jump!*" Jake yelled, and the others needed no further prompting.

As one, Oneiri Team leapt, their powerful legs carrying them dozens of meters into the air.

Jake slammed into the cliff face, and his implant simulated the air getting knocked out of his lungs, while he viewed the rock in front of him through a haze of maroon.

He scrabbled against the cliff side for a handhold, and when he couldn't find one, he drove his metal fingers into the rock, creating one.

Meanwhile, a piercing keen cut through the pain, and he realized this was an additional effort by the dream to convey the danger, as well as the damage that had already been done to his machine.

Well, that's new. At least the implant was coordinating with his subconscious to keep things fresh inside the dream.

He took a moment to glance around at his team, making sure everyone had managed to latch onto the cliff.

Ash had landed just above him, and now she dangled from one hand while scrabbling against the rock to find lodging for the other. *Sure hope she doesn't fall.* If she did, she'd come down right on top of him.

Marco was below him and to his left, and just beyond Marco, Beth clung to the rock.

Jake looked to his right. *There's Richaud. And Henrietta.* For an instant, he wondered where Tommy was, then he remembered with a pang that he was dead.

Where's Chief Roach?

He looked down. Roach had managed to make the jump, and he'd found purchase on the cliff face, too. But he'd landed far below the rest of Oneiri Team—only around half as high.

The Quatro had also leapt, and while most of them had failed to cling to the rock, two of them remained on it—both of them on narrow ledges not far below Roach.

One of them was attempting to claw its way up the rock, long, wicked claws taking shape as they were needed. The quad drove those newly formed claws into the cliff, pulled itself up, then did the same with its other front paw, using its back paws to stabilize itself.

It would soon reach Roach.

Captain Bob Bronson appeared beside Jake on the cliff, seeming to stand on nothing.

"Price. Thought I'd drop by to let you know my destroyer's in position. Feel free to launch whenever you, uh...whenever you find a good surface to launch from."

"Thanks, Captain," Jake said.

The quad reached Roach, then, surging upward to swipe at him with a giant paw. It succeeded in knocking Roach's mech from the cliff, and the chief tumbled toward the ground below.

Jake released his grip on the rock, pushing himself off slightly to the left as he plummeted.

A counter appeared along the top-center of his vision, calculating his acceleration due to Eresos' gravity.

He ignored it, focusing instead on Roach's MIMAS. The mech quickly grew larger in the visual feed from Jake's left foot, which he was patching through to his HUD.

Jake reached Gabe just before the quads on the ground did. He seized the commander of Oneiri Team, wrapping both arms tightly around Roach's mech, and he engaged his rockets.

The two of them launched toward the sky together, while below, the quads came together where Roach had lain.

CHAPTER 31

This Thing Is Moving

Despite Ellis's continued jokes, Peter could tell that both he and Noah were on edge since their strange discovery on the last comet they'd worked on.

Even the jokes themselves were getting more strident and less funny. They were just Ellis's way of coping, Peter had come to realize, and so he tried to tolerate them as best he could, despite how annoying he found them.

But neither the fresh memory of the robot that had crawled from the ice nor Ellis's jokes could account for a fraction of the stress Peter experienced every second of every day.

Even when he managed to sleep, his dreams were dark, fevered things. The reason was that adenosarcoma had finally begun to win the fight it had waged with his daughter for years.

Peter's business was booming. With the war on Eresos, and the trouble on Alex, there was a backlog of people who suddenly wanted nothing more than to live on a comet, millions of miles away from the inner system. Peter had recently leased a fourth comet hopper, and all four were fully operational, meaning he developed four comets at a time, with all of the materials he needed to do so—another luxury he'd rarely enjoyed before the boon brought by the discovery of the mech he'd sold to Darkstream.

A booming business meant having enough to cover the exorbitant costs involved with getting Sue Anne the advanced medical procedures she needed, this far out in the Belt. He'd even sprung for an experimental treatment, fresh from the cutting edge of medical science. Sue Anne hadn't been a good candidate for the treatment, given her deteriorated health, and to convince the researchers to accept her into their program, Peter had had to grease their palms considerably—to the tune of quadruple the cost of what more traditional treatments cost him.

Despite everything he'd done, the specialists he'd paid to come out to the Belt to personally oversee Sue Anne's care now told him she had mere weeks to live, if that.

Upon learning the news, his wife had begged Peter to come home. "You have to be at your daughter's side..." Brianne hadn't quite been able to bring herself to say the words "when she dies."

"Sue Anne needs you," she said instead.

But Peter had refused. There was no chance he was coming back. Not yet, at any rate. If Sue Anne died, she would die with him in the harness, working as hard as he could to save her.

That way, his conscience would never be able to tell him that he hadn't done absolutely everything he could to save his daughter's life.

Something will change. The doctors will come up with something. They have to.

He didn't truly believe that, but it was what he told himself at night, to snatch what little sleep he was able to.

Now, he stood in the *Whale*'s bridge, watching on the small viewscreen as they approached the next comet slated for development.

Ellis joined him, and they both watched as the comet grew larger on the screen.

"What do you reckon they'll end up building here, boss?" Ellis asked. "Maybe a shopping mall, this time? A theme park, perhaps?"

That did make Peter smile. It would be a long time before the Steele System's economy was developed enough to support a shopping mall anywhere, let alone in the Belt.

"If you don't get suited up soon, you'd better hope they build an unemployment line there, Ellis."

Ellis stared at him, blinking. "Was that...was that a joke, boss?"

"Yes, Ellis. It was a joke."

"Ah. It was funny! Sorry. Not used to hearing those from you."

Peter felt his smile tighten up, and he said nothing else.

They donned their pressure suits, and this time, Peter did ask Ellis to triple-check his, while he performed the same service for his employee.

"Safety first, eh, boss?"

"That's right."

By now, he and his two employees had figured out their routine, as well as their division of labor. Without having to say anything, Peter and Ellis scouted a suitable spot to start drilling, deployed the hose, and extended the radar from the side of the *Whale.*

As for Noah, he remained inside and forgot to turn on the water harvester until Peter reminded him, which reliably delayed everything, every single time.

Peter really should have terminated Noah a while ago, but he didn't have the heart. The man had children of his own, back on Eresos, and Peter knew he sent most of his paychecks back to their village's council, so that they could bolster security.

Personally, if Peter had been in Noah's situation, he would have been working like a dog. Hell, he basically *was* in Noah's situation, and that was exactly what he was doing. But he supposed not everyone had the get-up-and-go that others did.

"Boss..."

It was Ellis, examining the results from the step-frequency scan.

"What is it this time?" Peter asked.

"I think you'd have a better look at this."

Ellis flicked the radar image over to Peter's HUD.

It showed a mech, which looked identical to the first one that Peter and Jake had found.

"*Boss!*" This time, urgency filled Ellis's voice. "Boss, I just had a look at an updated image of this thing, and it's in a different position. This thing is moving, boss!"

Ellis sent the second image over, and Peter reviewed it, nodding grimly.

"It's trying to escape. Our arrival must have activated it, somehow."

"What do we do?"

"We get off this comet right now, and we contact Captain Bronson. Let's move, Ellis." Peter widened the radio channel to include his other employee. "No need to join us, Noah. We're coming back in."

"Why, boss? Something wrong?"

"Don't worry about it. You just go back to sleep."

CHAPTER 32

Coma

Oneiri Team all stood around Roach's bed in the Valhalla sick bay that Darkstream kept reserved for its soldiers and trainees. Captain Bronson was here, too, hands folded in front of him, eyes glued to the sheet that covered Roach.

Roach was totally unresponsive—deep within a coma that the doctors said could be permanent. Nanobots were hard at work within him, but the technology did not yet exist to repair the sort of damage done to Roach's brain, which the blood loss had resulted in. Their only hope now was that his brain repaired the necessary connections for consciousness by itself, which the doctors said did happen in rare occasions.

Chief Roach had aged markedly, which Jake hadn't noticed before. Probably his injuries had accelerated his aging, but Jake knew another reason he hadn't noticed was how much time they all spent inside their mechs. Though Roach's face was as hard as it had ever been, his forehead had acquired more lines, and his short black hair now had a couple of gray streaks.

"Isn't there anyone we should call?" Beth Arkanian asked. "Family? Friends?"

Bronson shook his head. "Gabe wasn't related to anyone who came with Darkstream to the Steele System. Plus, he mostly kept to himself, outside his interactions with fellow soldiers." Bronson narrowed his eyes, as though he was thinking. "There was one..." He seemed to glance at Ash. "Never mind. There's nobody."

"What's the situation, down on Eresos, Captain?" Jake said.

That brought a sigh from Bronson. "Not great. The eight Quatro piloting those mechs—quads, you call them, right?— they've broken away from their brethren as well as their new Red Company friends, and they're crossing the Barrens with incredible speed. Tomlinson's mech is with them, presumably piloted by one of the mercenaries. The expectation is that they'll start razing villages the moment they encounter them."

"So, what's our response going to be?" Ash asked. "From what we've seen, the quads are far more powerful than the MI-MAS mechs. Just one of them alone nearly killed Chief Roach."

"You're going to go back down there and try your best. What else can we do? The alternative is to abandon the people of Eresos, and I'm sure none of you want that. I do have some good news. Based on our study of the Ambler that Chief Roach found after it was taken down by Quatro, we've worked out how to make lasers function within a planet's atmosphere, and your mechs are being outfitted with them as we speak."

"Well, that's something," Henrietta said. "Probably not near-ly enough, but something."

"Why couldn't we use them before?" Richaud asked.

Bronson shook his head. "I don't think I'm able to explain it. Something to do with the atmosphere."

Marco spoke up. "The problem with lasers in atmospheres has always been that thermal blooming heated the air around the laser and caused the beam to spread out too much, rendering it useless. I'm assuming the solution was to use adaptive optics technology. If you could figure out the correct distribution of mirrors, you could distort the laser beam in a way that canceled the effect of the atmospheric turbulence, tightening up the beam. Is that how they resolved it, Captain?"

"Um...I do recall R&D mentioning mirrors..."

They all fell silent, then, their eyes on Roach's inert form.

"Is his implant still intact?" Jake asked.

"I don't remember the doctors saying either way," Bronson said, "but I'd be very surprised if it wasn't. Even Zimmerman's implant was intact, after the alien mech folded inward to pulverize him. Why do you ask?"

"Well, the implant allowed him to control the mech through lucid. Maybe it will allow him to communicate with us in the same way."

Bronson was nodding. "It's worth a shot." He pointed toward an empty bed nearby. "Why don't you give it a try? Do you have any sedatives on you?"

"Always." Jake made his way to the bed and lay on top of it, popping one of the sedatives into his mouth as his head hit the pillow.

Soon, he was in lucid. By default, he had his implant set to drop him into a high-lucidity area first, so that he could calibrate the experience he would have while asleep, instead of having to screw around with it before going to bed.

He instructed his implant to connect him via lucid with Roach's implant. Soon, he found himself inside a tiny village that looked like it was on Eresos. There were bodies strewn all over the ground, most looking like they'd been torn apart by savage beasts, their clothes soaked red.

It didn't take long for Jake to find Chief Roach. He was standing in front of what looked like the nicest house in the village, staring at a young woman lying on the grass, who wore a bloodstained white dress.

"Chief?"

Roach looked up, his eyes underscored by dark blotches.

Taking care not to move too fast, Jake approached. "Who's that?" he asked, nodding at the woman.

Silence from Roach.

"She looks like Ash," Jake said.

"It's her sister," Roach said. "Her name was Jess Sweeney." The chief's shoulders rose and fell. "Don't tell Steam you found me here, okay?"

You mean, don't tell her you were in love with her sister? "Okay."

"Why are you here?"

"You're in a coma. Totally unresponsive. Don't you know that?"

Roach nodded. "Yeah. Again. Why are you here?"

"We... wanted to see whether we could talk to you."

"Surely you don't think I can go on being your leader? After this?"

"It's not just about that. We're all worried about you."

"You're wasting your time." The chief's eyes returned to Jess Sweeney's body. Then they met Jake's again. "You really want to help me?"

"Yes."

"Then you can carry my body to the mech you and your father found inside that comet. Put me inside of it."

For a long time, Jake simply returned the chief's stare with one of his own. Then, he exited lucid.

When he woke, the others were studying his face expectantly.

"What did he say?" Beth asked.

"He said he doesn't want to talk. To anyone."

Her face fell, and the rest of Oneiri team looked pretty dejected, too. Only Bronson didn't react.

The rest stuck around for an hour or so more, watching Roach's motionless body, seldom speaking. After that, they all started to leave, one by one.

At last, it was just Jake and Roach, as well as the three other soldiers occupying beds in the sick bay, none of whom seemed to be paying any attention to Jake.

He detached three separate tubes from the chief's body, causing the machinery around him to start beeping stridently. When Jake picked him up, the chief didn't feel as heavy as he'd expected him to.

Ignoring the beeping, as well as the soldier it had awoken, who was staring at Jake wearing a perplexed expression, Jake carried Chief Roach through the exit.

An empty wheelchair sat outside sick bay, and Jake lowered the chief into it, his head lolling back.

The hour was late. Jake barely encountered anyone as he rolled Roach across Valhalla Station. Mostly civilians.

One officer—Commander Stevens, Jake read from the man's nametag—stopped Jake before he entered Darkstream Research and Development.

"Where are you taking Chief Roach, son?"

"We've discovered he's responsive to lucid, sir, even from within his coma. I've been ordered to take him to R&D to see about developing an exoskeleton, in order to restore mobility to the chief." The lie was fairly close to the truth, and it rolled off of Jake's tongue. That *was* essentially what Roach had ordered him to do.

"At two in the morning?" Stevens said.

Jake shrugged. "I guess somebody works best during late hours. I just do what I'm told, sir."

"Very good. Carry on."

When Jake reached a hatch that required security clearance, he lifted Roach's hand to the biometric scanner, pressing it against the surface. For the retina scan, Jake hoisted the chief by his armpits and used his shoulder to nudge the man's face against the sensor.

Roach's biometrics got them all the way to the titanium-reinforced room that housed the alien mech, which had been repaired since the damage the chief was said to have done to it.

The alien mech didn't seem to discriminate when it came to who used it—not based on biometrics, anyway. When Jake placed his palm on the machine's right calf, the back opened, just as it had for Zimmerman and Roach both.

Hauling Roach's limp body up the ramp and stuffing it into the mech proved to be the most challenging part of the whole process. Once he succeeded, the ramp snapped upward, and Jake leapt clear just in time. He'd been anticipating something like that, and so he'd been ready.

He landed on his butt, sending a jolt of pain through his lower back. He sat there, staring up at the alien mech.

A few seconds later, the mech began to move, turning to stare down at Jake.

CHAPTER 33

That Which
Nullifies

Gabe was whole again.

For as long as the alien mech decided to let him live, he was whole.

"Are you... all right?" Price asked him. The kid was sitting on the floor of the titanium-reinforced room, looking up at him.

The boy who'd first joined Gabe's training program, so many months ago, had fleshed out into a well-muscled adult: a young man, whose eyes had seen more than they should have by now.

Although Gabe already sensed that he'd regained the capacity for speech, he remained silent. He instructed his implant to call up a map of Alpha Quadrant, and he set his mind to plotting a route between here and the nearest landing bay.

Got it.

He willed both of his arms to turn into cannons, the mech's scaled surface sliding and shifting to become what he wanted. That done, he pelted the wall with blast after powerful blast of pure energy until it melted away enough for him to fit through if he ducked.

Jake followed him into the corridor. "Sir, where are you going?"

If you're concerned about the answer, you probably shouldn't have brought me here.

Gabe strode through the station, not bothering to run. There was no one aboard Valhalla with the ability to stop him from doing what he intended to do, so he adopted a leisurely pace.

A voice mumbled to him inside the mech dream. For the first time, he noticed that the quality of this dream was different from the one he'd experienced while piloting his MIMAS. Sound seemed to echo, here, and even though everything had a slightly hazy quality to it, it also seemed more real.

But "real" wasn't quite the right word. The world had taken on a dire quality, and it reminded him of times when he'd been extremely tired, times when his own internal voice had seemed to scream inside his head.

This is life, now. Better get used to it.

The mumbling continued all the way to Landing Bay Alpha, though the words were indistinct, and Gabe wasn't particularly interested in making them out, anyway. Jake followed behind him, running to keep up.

Bet you're glad I made you do all that PT.

At last, Gabe passed through the wide, sweeping arch that led into the landing bay. Darkstream employees ran from their posts toward him, some of them waving their arms frantically, most of them shouting. Gabe didn't care to heed their words, either. The forms approaching him were small enough to seem totally insignificant.

He crossed the landing Bay at a measured pace, until he stood before the main airlock, which was designed to admit old UHF combat shuttles, much larger than most of the craft that visited and departed Valhalla.

"You must open the airlock," Gabe said, speaking for the first time since entering the alien mech. The way his voice filled the entire landing bay pleased him. "If you don't, I'll blast through the inner and outer doors, and you'll all die. Now—quickly, please."

"Sir," Jake shouted. "Don't do this."

Gabe turned around to face him. "What did you expect? Did you think I would remain on Valhalla? Maybe do some shopping? Dip my giant metal heels in the water at the Endless Beach?"

"I expected you to rejoin Oneiri. To work with us."

"I told you to leave me behind for the quads. You didn't, and now you have to live with that choice. Either way, it's probably best if you behave as though I'm dead." Turning to face the airlock once more, he roared, "if these doors don't open within ten seconds, they won't be there anymore." His arms morphed to form cannons once again.

The doors opened, parting slowly, majestically.

Gabe stepped forward into the opening. He considered warning them about what would happen to the outer doors if they refused to open them, but he decided it was probably already pretty obvious.

Inside the dream, the alien mech muttered again, and this time, Gabe could make out the words: *Is our union that which nullifies?*

"Yes," he answered as the outer doors drew apart to reveal the inky blackness of space. "I believe it is."

He jumped.

CHAPTER 34

Try Something Else

"They didn't just know you were still training the militia because we successfully defeated the prisoner uprising," Tessa said, glancing around the Dusty Bucket, where they were on their second drink. "They've been monitoring our lucid sessions—I'm sure of it."

Lisa nodded, still unable to believe that she no longer viewed this sort of talk as borderline insane.

It's all so crazy. Everything.

But she remembered the man she'd seen in one of their simulations. Plus, Laudano had seemed to wait for the perfect moment to spring on her the fact he knew she was still working with her militia.

What else is he keeping in his back pocket, to use against me when he has need of manipulating me again?

"What do you suggest?" she asked Tessa.

"Well, we need to talk, and I wouldn't be surprised if the streets themselves are bugged. The alleyways, too." Tessa nodded at the bar behind Lisa, her long white hair swaying forward.

"Darkstream definitely has this place bugged. Imagine the intel they'd collect from listening in on conversations here."

"So, what? Do we go outside Habitat 2?"

"No. Radio communications can easily be intercepted. We need to reenter lucid, just the two of us, and hash this thing out. We just need to put the proper security measures in place first."

For that, they went to Bob O'Toole, who, conveniently, was sitting on his customary stool at the bar.

"You have need of me, m'ladies?" O'Toole asked, his words coming out slurred.

"Need of your friends, more like," Lisa said, adopting the usual stern expression she used with O'Toole. The man had proved himself useful, but she still understood the need to keep him at arm's length. "We need a way to disguise net traffic between mine and Tessa's implant, maybe reroute it somehow."

"I don't know what most of that means, but I'll put in a good word for you to one of my nerds. Should I have them meet you somewhere?"

"My place," Tessa said. "And send a female, O'Toole."

As they made their way to Tessa's modest house, Lisa said, "If they're monitoring our communications as closely as we think they are, isn't it likely they just overheard that conversation?"

Tessa nodded. "Possible. But it's a gamble we need to take. They can't process all communications at all times. Probably they'll get around to listening to it eventually, but by then we'll have had our secret conversation, hopefully. And to prosecute us after the fact, they'd have to admit to spying."

Soon, with the help of a woman named Stacey Quick, they were inside lucid, in a realm that Quick assured them was secure.

"Okay," Lisa said, her hands folded on a table that Quick had graciously provided them with. "I assume you want to discuss preparations for dealing with Daybreak?"

"I do. And *I* can only assume that you're ready to start developing a defense plan that doesn't involve Darkstream. Because if you aren't, you can expect to lose Habitat 2. It wasn't a coincidence that the company operatives were all out 'scouting the terrain' while the prisoners got loose. I'd go as far to say that I bet Laudano furnished them with the keycard, or delegated someone else to do it, so he didn't have to get his hands dirty."

"What do you think they were really doing out on Alex, then?"

"If I were to bet? Looking for Rug and the others."

That sent a shiver through Lisa. "Thank God they didn't find them."

"Indeed."

"Well, I've seen enough to start thinking it's far likelier that you're right about Darkstream than wrong. I trust your judgment, Tessa."

"You didn't trust it enough. Not until now. If you had, we'd be better prepared for this."

Lisa pressed her lips together. "You're right," she said at last. "I apologize."

"It's...fine," Tessa said slowly, with a small shake of her head. "You haven't seen what I've witnessed Darkstream do. You don't know the extent of what they're capable of."

"What did you see, Tessa? What did you witness them do?"

"Hopefully I can tell you, one day. But that day is not yet here."

Lisa studied the older woman's face—the deep lines that crisscrossed it. Worry lines, stress lines. "You're afraid of Darkstream, aren't you, Tessa?"

"Yes," Tessa said, without hesitation. "You should be, too."

Lisa nodded, and then she sighed. "Unfortunately, I don't think Habitat 2 can be saved."

That seemed to give Tessa pause, and the white-haired woman blinked. "We have to try."

"I agree...that we should try. But I've been giving this a lot of thought, and as much as it kills me to say it...I think we should try something else."

CHAPTER 35

All the Cards

Everyone in Landing Bay Alpha had overheard Jake's conversation with Chief Roach before the man had jumped to the planet below.

It would have been impossible not to. Jake had been shouting, and Roach...well, Roach's voice had seemed to shake the entire station.

It was also incredibly easy to piece together that Jake was responsible for transporting Chief Roach to the alien mech and placing him inside it. The security footage was all there, in addition to the conversation overheard by the flight deck crew. Commander Stevens had seen him wheeling Roach through Alpha Quadrant.

His insubordinate act could be pinned to him in at least three different ways. He supposed he'd hoped that this would end up being one of those insubordinate acts that turned out for the best, and for which everyone praised him.

I didn't expect Roach to behave like he did.

So it didn't surprise him when Captain Bronson summoned him to his office.

"Seaman Price," the captain said from behind an enormous mahogany desk. "Take a seat."

That *did* surprise him, a little. Jake hadn't expected to be permitted to sit.

"How are you, son?" Bronson asked. "A bit shaken up, I expect?"

"A bit, sir."

"Completely understandable. But you'll be back to normal soon. I need you to be, anyway."

"Uh...yes, sir," Jake said cautiously, unsure about when Bronson would begin outlining all of the consequences he'd face.

Bronson sighed, lacing his fingers behind his head and leaning back in his reclining chair. "You know, son, until very recently, Eresos was a tremendous growth market for Darkstream. The renewed Quatro threat were driving contracts like crazy, making them multiply magically. They doubled over an extremely short time—tripled, even! Not only that, the rates we were able to negotiate went way up. It was a bonanza, Price. And now, with these quads, as you call them, and Red Company allying with the Quatro..." Bronson shook his head. "Can you see the problem, son?"

"Uh, yes, sir. The people of Eresos are starting to see us as weak. We can't hide how we were forced by the quads to abandon the surface. And with the quads as their allies, Red Company can start extorting massive fees, for protection."

"That's very perceptive, son. Very perceptive."

"Well...Marco broke it down for me, mostly, sir."

"Ah. Then I must say, it takes character to give credit where it's due, especially when you don't have to. You pilot your mech like a pro, Price. That's all Darkstream has ever needed from you."

"Yes, sir."

"Anyway. What I'm getting at is that Darkstream is very keen to stabilize the situation on Eresos, to decisively neuter this new threat posed by the quads, and to get back to a place of growth. We're hoping Chief Roach will help with that effort, and not hinder it, inside that new alien monstrosity of his. Hopefully he won't end up getting himself killed, like Zimmerman did. But he's a wild card, now, and we can't factor him into our plans, so we'll put him out of mind for now."

Jake coughed into his curled fist. "Um, sir...you do know that I'm the one who carried Chief Roach to R&D, right?"

"Yes, yes. But I'd assumed he ordered you to do it. Did he not?"

"Well, yes, sir."

"Then you were only following orders. If anyone did something wrong, it was Roach, not you. True, he deprived us of the ability to continue studying the thing—we'd only just begun to learn its secrets—but that's not your fault."

Jake nodded slowly. The fact that Bronson was taking it so easy on him made him suspect the man needed him for something, and so it was simpler not to discipline him.

I wonder if Bronson knows how transparent he is. Probably, it didn't matter either way. Bronson held all the authority, all the cards. Any maneuvering from him now was likely meant to ensure Jake followed orders as enthusiastically as possible.

Bronson was smiling at him, in a way Jake assumed the man thought was comforting, but the silence was getting a bit awkward in its length.

"I'll do what I can to resolve the situation on Eresos, sir," Jake said at last.

"Eresos? Oh, you're not going back down to Eresos, son."

"I-I'm not?"

"No, no. You're going back to the Belt."

Another silence ensued, but Jake broke this one a lot sooner than the first: "The Belt, sir?" He cleared his throat. So, he was being disciplined for taking the chief to the alien mech after all. A jolt of fear ran through his body at the thought that he was about to lose his place on Oneiri Team.

Nodding, Bronson said, "Your father just found another mech encased in a comet. Only difference is that this one has activated, and it's currently attempting to escape. Who knows what it'll do once it succeeds. Your father has backed away from it, but we still don't know what these things are truly capable of, and so we aren't going to take any chances. You're coming with me, in the *Javelin*, and together we'll either take it in or neutralize it if we can't."

This time, Jake's fear manifested as a ball of ice in the pit of his stomach rather than a jolt through his body.

Dad.

Peter Price was in danger—possibly, everyone living in the Belt was in danger.

"I'm in, sir. When do we leave?"

"Right now." Bronson stood up, his grin widening, which Jake found fairly off-putting. "Follow me."

CHAPTER 36

Oxygen

Lisa stood with her fellow Darkstream operatives on the roof of Habitat 2 when the Daybreak force rolled up.

Before the battle, Quentin Cooper had requested parlay with Laudano, who stood near the edge of Habitat 2's roof, in plain sight. As agreed beforehand, Cooper also stood in full view, so that both commanders were taking on equal risk.

Upon Cooper's first appearance, Lisa had instructed her implant to zoom in to confirm his identity through his faceplate, just as she was sure her colleagues had as well.

At least, I hope they did.

Cooper's force had approached from the west—the same direction Lisa, Andy, Tessa, and the Quatro had approached during their attack, months ago.

As for the composition of Cooper's force, it seemed Leonardo Fiore had been telling the truth. Between the reinforcements he'd gained from his contacts in Habitat 1, along with the forces he must have had hidden in Alex's wilderness, away from the major supply routes, Cooper had two hundred soldiers under his command, as well as eight beetles, all of which had been modified for war.

As far as the weaponry wielded by Cooper's people went, Lisa spotted at least four rocket launchers, plus a smattering of sniper rifles, shotguns, and plenty of assault rifles, though those wouldn't prove very useful unless Daybreak managed to penetrate Habitat 2.

Which Lisa fully expected they would.

An intelligent defense would have rooftop snipers picking off Cooper's rocket launcher-bearing soldiers first, followed by as many snipers as Laudano could manage to neutralize. Meanwhile, Lisa would have had Darkstream's own rocket launchers targeting the beetles, before they did too much damage to the structure of Habitat 2.

But Lisa wasn't confident Laudano intended to conduct an intelligent defense.

Cooper spoke first, over the wide channel they'd decided on for their parlay: "You can't win, Commander." Lisa was reminded of a play put on by school children, which she'd seen back in the Belt, right before she'd left to work for Darkstream. They'd been reenacting a battle from the Milky Way's First Galactic War, if she recalled correctly. "My forces are too great," Cooper went on. "We intend to blow open Habitat 2 and retake it for our own."

"Just try it," Laudano said, and his acting came across as a little more natural.

Even so, Lisa could see it for what it was, now: acting, and bad acting at that. Now that she'd come around to Tessa's way of thinking, the truth seemed glaringly obvious to her, shining brightly from behind everything Laudano said or did.

"I'll give you one chance to leave Habitat 2 without losing any of your people," Cooper said. "Take it, or die."

"We'll never let you oppress the people of this city again," Laudano said. "Get ready for war, Cooper."

"Very well," Cooper said, turning to walk toward the valley, to where it had been agreed all of the Daybreak forces would return before the battle began.

Then, predictably, Cooper broke his word. He leapt behind one of the beetles and gave the order to start firing.

His soldiers moved behind the vehicles, too, also taking cover there, while Cooper's snipers fired on the Darkstream soldiers on Habitat 2's roof.

For their part, the Darkstream combat operatives scrambled for cover of their own, Commander Laudano included.

Laudano let *this happen. It's all so transparent.*

Indeed, the battle was unfolding exactly as Tessa had predicted.

Keeping an eye on the Darkstream soldiers nearest her, Lisa crept quietly backward, toward the nearest rooftop airlock, where she intended to take a freight elevator back down into the city.

The beetles started firing, then, and before Lisa managed to reach the freight elevator, she heard over a wide channel: "They've blown a hole in the side of the habitat!"

The panic Lisa heard in the soldier's voice sounded genuine.

Maybe the lower-ranking soldiers aren't in on it.

That seemed likely, now that she thought about it. If it had been otherwise, the chances would have been much greater of Laudano's plan leaking.

It also meant that innocent men and women would die today. But that had been inevitable no matter what happened.

Lisa reached the airlock, palming the controls, her stomach tense as she waited for the outer doors to open. When they did, she crept inside, slapping the biometric scanner once again to close the outer doors and then to open the inner ones.

At last, she was alone inside the elevator. As it descended, another message came—this time, from the elevator's overhead speaker. That meant it was being broadcast throughout all of Habitat 2.

It was Laudano: "The habitat has been breached. All residents, go directly to your homes, seal the entrance, and activate emergency life support until the situation is resolved. I repeat, all residents, go directly to your homes."

The elevator doors opened onto the streets of Habitat 2, which had already descended into chaos, with residents scrambling through the streets as the oxygen they breathed was sucked out of the city by the breach.

Lisa kept her pressure suit on. She headed for the Dusty Bucket.

CHAPTER 37

Billy's Bunker

When the other inhabitants of River Rock saw the cloud rising up over the Barrens, they called it just another dust storm—a fixture of life on the border between Eresos' wetlands and the Barrens, where one became the other with an abruptness you rarely would have seen back on Old Earth.

"Nope," Billy Overton said, his thumbs tucked behind his belt. "That's no dust storm." He'd seen plenty of those during his sixty-five years, and this wasn't one.

Dust storms came in like giant, puffy clouds rising up from the ground. This dust-up was narrower, high, and sharp.

"Those are machines coming," Billy said out loud, though no one had stuck around to hear him say it. As usual. "Big ones. And fast." The others had already decided that the oncoming formation was a dust storm, though, and so now they were in dust-storm mode. "Sure hope they're friendly, those machines. Else the rest of you's in for a mighty surprise. Ah, yes."

Billy didn't plan on sticking around to gauge the friendliness of the machines for himself. Instead, he meant to head for the bunker he'd paid Darkstream to install for him, right underneath his front yard.

You never knew when you might need a bug-out shelter in your front yard when you lived on a planet populated by giant aliens who could snap your shins clean in two with a single munch. Especially when your town council was too cheap to sign a security contract, not even with those ragtag mercenaries that had set up shop recently.

Billy Overton never needed much of an excuse to hunker down in his shelter. Sometimes, he even went down there if he wanted to pretend he wasn't home, like when that insufferable Sable Hawthorne came calling. The others were used to him heading for it, so even if they noticed he was doing so now, that wouldn't serve them as a tip-off of approaching danger, either.

"Tried to warn you," Billy said to himself as he ambled toward his property, which he was already only a stone's throw away from. He knew they thought of him as the old man who cried wolf, and they considered his version of crying wolf to be hunkering down in that shelter of his.

Well, someday calamity really will come. Then I'll get my money's worth, damn it. And you lot will be sorry.

He fumbled his keycard out of his pocket, hands trembling slightly—as they always did, ever since the accident with the farm robot a half-dozen years ago—and he made his way around the side of the house to caress the scanner with the card.

It didn't open. Grumbling, he cursed under his breath about what a cheap product it was as he wiped it off on his shirt and tried again.

This time, it worked, the tiny hatch sliding open and a cheery voice greeting him with a "Hello, Billy," its voice sounding a little tinny by now, after such repeated use.

"Hello yourself," Billy said as he lowered himself carefully down the ladder and closed the hatch behind him.

Ah, yes. Security. Solitude. He put on a cup of joe and booted up the vid stream from the street in front of his house.

Quiet, so far. *Probably nothing again.* It was always nothing. Sometimes, he cursed himself for buying this fool shelter from Darkstream. He never would have admitted that to anyone, but down here in its confines, he did permit himself such thoughts.

Here came Sable Hawthorne, hobbling down the dusty lane, beating at patches of grass with her cane.

Tens of thousands of credits gone, all for the privilege of watching crusty old Sable Hawthorne hobble down the road at two inches an hour.

Billy knew the Amblers malfunctioned sometimes, deviating from their preprogrammed routes, but none had ever come rampaging through here, of course. No, that would have justified Billy's purchase. *Can't have that.*

He sighed, long and ragged, the kind of exhalation that he'd never permit himself around the other inhabitants of River Rock. He settled into the shelter's single seat with the fresh coffee.

At least I have this, he said, raising the mug to his lips.

Without warning, a great metal monstrosity came out of nowhere, knocking Sable Hawthorne clean off the screen.

Billy leapt to his feet, coffee spilling all over him, and he danced around the shelter, shouting and waving his arms. "Ah! Ah! Ah!"

At last, he regained the presence of mind to strip off his shirt, though he expected he hadn't succeeded in sparing himself a bad burn. It had already begun to sting across his stomach and chest.

He returned his attention to the screen, and he grasped the joystick that manipulated the camera affixed to the roof of his house, jerking it to the left. His smarting gut hung out over his belt, and as the camera slowly shifted, he patted the forming welt gingerly.

There. There she was. Sable lay on the ground, her cane nowhere in sight, her face a ruined, bloody mess.

Billy's eyes went so wide they ached. "Oh my God," he muttered, his voice getting real high-pitched on the last word.

Somehow, he felt none of the satisfaction he'd always expected to feel in the event of a calamitous event striking River Rock. Not only that, he experienced a sharp pang of guilt over all the nasty things he'd thought about Sable Hawthorne over the years.

Poor old woman. She's dead.

He took hold of the joystick once again, directing the camera toward the village green. "Come on," he muttered as the view shifted at a glacial pace. "Come on..."

There.

"Wow," he whispered.

There the monster was that had taken down Sable, shooting great blasts of energy all over the place, at every building in sight. All around it were armed men and women, gunning down the residents of River Rock like they were cutting the grass, and to top it all off, a troop of six Quatro were rampaging around town, too.

This wasn't just calamity. This was the apocalypse, as far as Billy was concerned. And even if he made it through—even if his shelter really could withstand those balls of energy, which obliterated entire walls and set structures instantly ablaze—Billy realized he wouldn't have a soul left to talk to. He'd never much been interested in chitchat, before, but the realization that he might lose the opportunity altogether made him feel sad.

Another metal monstrosity strode onto the village green, then, appearing around a building that the first monster had turned into an inferno. This one had two legs, instead of the four that the first one had.

I doubt that makes a difference. They look mighty similar. Now they'll just do twice the damage.

It was that thinking that made him so surprised when the second monster squared off with the first, and they seemed to size each other up for a moment before running at one another at top speed.

The new mech brought both its hands together, and they melded together to form a giant drill-shape. It rammed that straight into the four-legged monster's chest, sending it crashing backward into one of the buildings it had already set alight.

That done, the new monster turned on the armed humans, making short work of them in a fireworks display of explosive rounds and energy blasts.

The ranks of humans ravaged in a matter of seconds, the newcomer turned on the Quatro, blasting one of them to pieces before turning twin cannons on another.

Then, the four-legged metal monster recovered, bounding right out of its fiery handiwork to charge at the two-legged monster once more.

But the two-legged one was having none of it. Its right arm seemed to gather together into an over-sized fist, the mass of its bicep and forearm transitioning right to the front of its arm. Then it socked the four-legged machine right in the kisser, *pow,* and the thing went flying again.

It had had enough, this time. The thing bellowed, scampering out of town, and the Quatro left alive by the two-legged monster followed, along with three of the human attackers who could still run, though the victorious mech picked those three off before they left the green.

Billy turned to run through his shelter, key open the hatch, and dash through the village, toward the site of the battle.

"Hey, thanks!" he bawled, but by then the two-legged monster was just a speck on the horizon, running like lightning in the direction of Ingress.

CHAPTER 38

Slave State

Every building in Habitat 2 was outfitted with a temporary airlock that extended from the entrance to form an enclosure just inside. When Lisa reached the Dusty Bucket, Phineas Gage opened the regular door for her to reveal the baggy, plastic compartment that would prevent all of the oxygen from rushing out into the streets, which were quickly emptying of air, thanks to the giant hole blown in the side of the habitat by Daybreak.

"Can I get you something to drink?" Phineas Gage asked her as she emerged from the plastic cocoon.

"Very funny." The others had dragged a bunch of tables together to form a long shape that roughly resembled a rectangle. It was odd, seeing Phineas on this side of the bar, especially wearing a pressure suit indoors, as they all were, though no one had their helmets on. Quickly surveying those gathered, Lisa said, "looks like everyone's here?"

"Yes, ma'am," Bob O'Toole said, hiccuping.

Lisa glanced sharply at Phineas. "You didn't let him get into the booze, did you?"

"He certainly didn't," O'Toole said, actually sounding affronted. "That was an innocent hiccup."

"That would be a first." Gunfire sounded outside, fairly close by, but it didn't sound like enough. She would have expected a battle for the control of an entire habitat to be a little livelier than this. Turning to Andy, Lisa said, "Have you been able to access the security feeds?"

Andy shook his head. "Looks like they have the clearance required jacked up too high. They let you keep your M-level clearance, right?"

"They did." Darkstream certainly hadn't rewarded her for retaking Habitat 2 from Daybreak, but it would've been pretty lousy for them to downgrade her security clearance for her efforts. "I'll access the feeds and patch it through to your implants and v-lenses so we can all see what's going on out there."

Lisa did as she said she would, and what they ended up witnessing struck her as pretty sad.

Outside, in the streets of Habitat 2, the pressure suit-clad Darkstream soldiers appeared to be engaging their 'enemy' halfheartedly, firing spastically at the Daybreak fighters that poured into the city. The Darkstream soldiers weren't shy about falling back, retreating at the slightest opposition, ceding ground willingly.

Maybe all of the Darkstream combat operatives are *in on Laudano's plan.* Either that, or Laudano had explicitly told them that their own lives were far more important than preserving those of Habitat 2's residents, and that they should give up on everything except the perfect engagement.

"This is nothing but a performance for our benefit," Tessa said. "To buy time."

"Time for what?" Phineas Gage said.

"Time for smoothly transitioning control of Habitat 2 to Quentin Cooper. Time to reestablish their slave state with as little fuss as possible."

"No way," Phineas said. "I'm a free man. I can come and go as I please from my own bar."

"If that's the case," Tessa said, "why don't you go inside the temporary airlock, seal it up behind you, and try opening that outer door? If I'm right, Darkstream will have put the entire city on emergency lockdown by now, preventing anyone from leaving their homes to interfere with their plan."

Phineas met her gaze for a long moment, and then, grim-faced, he donned his pressure suit's helmet and headed for the airlock.

He sealed it behind him, and evacuated the oxygen from it before trying the door.

"You're right," he said over their militia-wide channel. "It's locked."

Tessa's gaze now rested on Lisa's face, and Lisa knew the meaning of it. This was confirmation of everything the older woman had always said about Darkstream. Their final betrayal was happening before their eyes, and all the citizen militia could do was hope that their preparations would be enough.

CHAPTER 39

Play with Explosives

Phineas Gage slowly unzipped the temporary airlock and stepped out, looking downtrodden. His eyes found Lisa's.

"Could you...could you try using your clearance to open the door?"

Lisa nodded, donning her helmet. They traded places, with Lisa inside the temporary airlock, zipping it up and waiting for the oxygen to get pumped back into the Dusty Bucket.

Lisa thought she knew why Phineas was having trouble accepting that he'd lost control over the door to his own establishment. It didn't just mean losing the illusion of control—it also meant that he likely wouldn't be able to go on doing business. Not in Habitat 2, anyway.

It meant that Darkstream, the company everyone depended on for pretty much everything, wasn't trustworthy. Even though the militia had been preparing for exactly this situation, it was still difficult to accept. Lisa was certainly still having trouble accepting it. She felt like everything she'd come to count on and cherish had fallen apart.

When she tried opening the door of the Dusty Bucket, it wouldn't, and she received an alert on her HUD that said: "ACCESSING THAT COMMAND REQUIRES A U-LEVEL CLEARANCE OR HIGHER." Commander Laudano was almost certainly the only person in all of Habitat 2 with clearance that high.

So Tessa was definitely right. *Time to accept it—truly accept it.* Darkstream was helping Daybreak to set up the slave colony they'd failed to maintain before.

Unzipping the temporary airlock, Lisa rejoined the others inside.

"How will Darkstream try to spin this, to the rest of the system?" she asked Tessa.

The older woman's lips formed a thin line. "My guess? They'll leave Habitat 2 altogether, and put it out that they were 'defeated' by Daybreak. The inhabitants will have their system net access cut again, anyway, so no one will be able to contradict their narrative."

Lisa carefully lowered herself into a seat once again, staring at the bar's floor, which, true to its namesake, was in need of sweeping. "I still can't understand how they're able to justify this."

"It's not about justifying it," Tessa said. "It's inevitable. Darkstream is by far the most powerful entity in the Steele System, so it's *inevitable* that they would continue to expand, and that, increasingly, they would have to do awful things to achieve that continued expansion."

"But why do they need to keep expanding? Why can't they just be happy with the money they're making?"

Tessa adjusted her white hair so that it hung forward over her left shoulder. "Growth and expansion is the whole reason corporations exist. Back in the Milky Way, when we were still subject to laws, being a corporation meant being legally obligated to place short-term shareholder profit growth above every other concern. And even though Darkstream is no longer *legally* obligated to try to continually increase profits, they aren't built to do anything else, either. It's in their DNA to subordinate everything to growth. And one of the best and quickest way to grow is to steal from another group of people. That's what's happening here on Alex. Habitat 2 is just a test case. The other habitats will be next."

Every word Tessa spoke made Lisa angrier, and at last, she'd heard enough. "Well, that's why we have a contingency plan," she said, harsher than she'd meant to. "Vickers, set the charge."

"Yes, ma'am!" Rodney Vickers said.

He's finally getting his chance to play with explosives. "Andy, contact Rug to make sure she and the other Quatro are in position."

"Yes, ma'am."

Once the charge was set, Lisa ordered everyone in her militia into the basement of the Dusty Bucket.

Other than the fact that it was owned by Phineas, the Bucket's basement was one of the main reasons they'd chosen this place as a launching pad to effect their plan. That, and its relative proximity to two different beetle bays—they hadn't been sure which they would need to access when the time came, as it depended on Daybreak's angle of attack.

Soon, everyone was crowded in the basement, wearing their full pressure suits.

"Blow it, O'Toole," Lisa said.

The roar of an explosion sounded above them, causing the whole structure to shake.

CHAPTER 40

More Hectic than Expected

Jake paced the *Javelin*'s shuttle bay in his MIMAS, metal feet *clanking* across the deck. He'd requested that Bronson patch the visual sensor feed through to his HUD for him to access at will, and now he monitored a zoomed-in view of the comet as they approached.

The alien mech had already freed itself from the ice, and now it strode back and forth across the surface, as though waiting for Jake's arrival.

He knew his father's ship was still in the neighborhood, and he worried about whether the alien mech had the means to leave the comet, if it wanted to. Probably, it did. On the way here, Bronson had briefed him on the smaller robot his father had uncovered, which had launched itself deeper into the Belt under its own power, before Peter Price could do anything to stop it. The *Whale*'s sensors had captured the thing's likeness—its thin, diminutive frame and its dark gray, shield-like limbs.

The mech he was about to fight could likely do the same thing, if it wished. Either way, it remained on the ice, for now.

You know I'm coming for you, don't you?

A vid call pinged his HUD, and when he saw the name, Jake's breath caught in his throat, which he wouldn't have expected.

Peter Price appeared before him, seeming to stand on the *Javelin*'s deck. "Jake," he said.

"Dad," Jake said, looking down at him, fighting to keep his voice level. His HUD told him his father's comet hopper was at least keeping its distance from the comet, in case the alien mech decided to attack.

"You've grown, son. I can see it in your eyes, and I can hear it in your voice."

"Thank you," Jake said, pausing, suddenly unsure what to say to his father. So much had happened since they'd last spoken, and Peter was right—he *had* changed. "Have you heard from mom?" he said at last. "I haven't gotten any updates from Hub in a while."

"Sue Anne is stable...for now," Peter said, his voice trailing off on the last words.

Jake nodded, not trusting himself to speak.

Peter sighed. "What has Darkstream had you do for them, Jake? How many have they had you kill?"

The question caught Jake off guard, and he shook his head slowly. "I've been fighting the Quatro, Dad. Protecting the people of Eresos."

"We never should have had to fight the Quatro. Things might have been different. We might have had peace."

"How?"

Peter hesitated. "Never mind. You don't need to hear this, right now. You're about to go up against that...thing. It's just that I feel badly about ever agreeing to let Bronson talk to you, after we found the first mech."

"It was my choice to accept his offer, Dad. You couldn't keep it from me forever."

"I know. I just felt like I was..." Peter shook his head. "Never mind. Fight well, son. And come back in one piece."

"I will. I promise. Bye, Dad." Jake willed the conversation away, and his father vanished from the destroyer. Jake was glad for it to be over. It was good to speak with his father again, but he hadn't expected it to be so intense, and he needed to prepare mentally for the coming fight.

Bronson contacted him next, looking surprisingly calm. *I guess he's been in plenty of battles.* Plus, he wasn't the one who had to leave the destroyer to go face that thing.

"This should be fairly straightforward," Bronson said.

Easy for you to say. But Jake didn't comment.

"Just land and set off the EMP—don't wait for that thing to try anything. Remember, the EMP only has one charge, so don't screw it up. It'll shut down your mech, too, so once you activate it, just wait for us to come get you. The EMP's strong enough to shut down systems critical to functioning in both mechs, but not strong enough to damage every system, so both should be fairly straightforward to repair afterward, including the alien mech, if we want to repair that. We've already tested this on the mech

Gabe made off with, so we know it works. Once you execute, we'll take both mechs aboard and call it a day."

"Yes, sir."

"We're drawing up beside the comet now. I'll open up the shuttle bay, and you jump out. Don't screw up the jump, for God's sake. If things go south after you land, we'll hit that thing with the *Javelin*'s weapons until we've got it under control. There really shouldn't be very much to this, Price."

"Yes, sir." In front of Jake's MIMAS, the shuttle bay doors had begun to open. Jake stepped forward, getting into position and crouching slightly. The EMP device was affixed to the side of his mech.

All I have to do is set it off.

When the doors drew apart, he leapt.

On the surface of the comet, the alien mech reacted immediately. Luckily, the thing chose to go with a pair of rockets to try to shoot Jake on his way over, and Jake responded by retracting his hands and pelting the missiles with his rotary autocannons. He neutralized them both well before they reached him, and they became brief flashes in the void.

Then his feet hit the ice surface, and the alien mech charged.

Of course, charges didn't amount to much, in the incredibly low gravity of the comet. Jake sidestepped with ease, taking care not to send himself careening into space.

The mech *did* leave the comet's surface, but only briefly. It spread its hands backward, igniting thrusters that blossomed from its palms to return to the comet's surface.

Jake fired the autocannons again, and the momentum pushed the MIMAS backward across the ice.

Screw this. It was time to activate the EMP. He placed a giant metal hand over the device, ready to activate it as soon as the alien mech drew near.

"Price!" It was Bronson, and this time he *did* sound panicked.

Jake turned to stare back at the destroyer. An enormous cloud of tiny robots had appeared, presumably from the closest comet, which had drawn suspiciously near. The robots were now sailing toward the warship, and the ones in front were about to land on her hull.

The *Javelin* was using secondary lasers, kinetic impactors, and missiles to try to take down as many of the robots as she could, and several went down, but there were a lot more where that came from. At least half of the robots looked set to land on the ship.

The destroyer's point defense turrets were the last line of defense, and they took down a few more of the robots. Then, the first ones landed. When they did, they started plunging their metal hands into the *Javelin*'s surface, ripping away at the steel as though it were tissue paper.

"Sir!" Jake said. "Is she going to be all right?"

"We have no way to deal with the ones that landed!" Bronson said. "Price—don't set off that EMP yet. I need your mech operational, in order to pick off these things!"

Inside the dream, the midnight-black of space flashed red and white. Jake looked at the mech, which was still charging, and then back at the tinier robots, industriously savaging the *Javelin.*

With creeping fear, he began to appreciate just how desperate his situation had become: he'd have to somehow fend off the alien mech while dealing with the robots attacking the destroyer.

He shook himself. *Better get to work.* He opened fire with the rotary autocannons, and the rounds' momentum pushed him backward across the ice once more.

"Dad, take the *Whale* farther out," he yelled over a wide channel. "This is going to be more hectic than expected!"

CHAPTER 41

Paste

With Chief Roach gone native, and Jake haring off to the Belt, Ash Sweeney found herself in command of what remained of Oneiri Team.

Of course, she herself was under the command of Captain Arkady Black, who had been picked up by a shuttle from Plenitos and flown to Valhalla Station in time to command the new reserve battalion Darkstream was sending down to Eresos, to try to stop the quads, Quatro, and Red Company.

The soldiers of this reserve battalion called themselves the Winged Dragons.

What is it with Darkstream reserve forces and awful names? All dragons have wings. The name was woefully redundant, though Ash supposed it did roll off the tongue.

Leaving her mech where it sat near the others, she paced around the space elevator as it inched toward the planet, with painful slowness. Weaving between infantry, tanks, and personnel carriers, Ash wondered whether Captain Black actually had a plan for beating the Quatro that was likely to work. If he did, he hadn't shared it with her.

I guess OPSEC is a thing.

She ran over the names of the MIMAS pilots now under her command, as well as each pilot's main strength, as far as battle was concerned.

Richaud—bold. Marco—quick-witted. Henrietta—dogged. Beth...

Ash rounded a tank, and suddenly Beth Arkanian was before her, wearing her characteristic warm smile.

"Hey, Steam."

"Hey...Paste," Ash said, making a snap decision.

"Paste?"

"Yeah. You keep us together, Beth. I don't know if you're ever going to get a nickname from battle, because your best quality is the way you keep us together *outside* of battle, like glue. You keep us all on the level, ready for the next engagement. So, Paste."

"Okay, then. Paste it is. Thanks."

"How are you holding up?" Ash said.

"I came here to ask you the same thing."

Ash nodded. "Just like paste would."

"I'm pretty sure paste can't talk," Beth said. "I get your meaning, though. How are you, Steam?"

"I'm, uh..." Ash shook her head. "I'm not sure."

"Anything you want to talk about?"

Kind of. She couldn't stop thinking about what Jake had told her before he left for the Belt. But he'd told her because he thought she deserved to know. It wasn't her place to spread gossip about the chief, even if he *had* jumped from a space station inside an alien mech while in a coma. "Nah. Just getting used to the idea of command, I guess."

"Well, I'm always there for you, if you need me."

"I know you are. Thanks, Paste."

Beth smiled wider, then turned and headed back toward the mechs, pinned brown hair bobbing behind her.

Maybe Paste isn't a great nickname. Oh well.

Her thoughts returned to what Jake had told her before leaving for the Belt—about Chief Roach and Ash's sister, Jess.

It had been so unexpected. She'd remembered Jess writing her about a new man in her life, an older man, who she'd claimed to be obsessed with. "I'm going to make a move on him soon," Jess had written. Ash never would have guessed that the man was Gabriel Roach.

Apparently, Jess's move had panned out—at least, according to what Jake had seen when he'd entered lucid to speak with Roach.

"He loved her, Ash," Jake had said. "There's no question about that."

The age difference between her sister and Roach had been quite large, but Jess had always gone after what she wanted, regardless of anyone's opinion. Ash didn't begrudge her that, and she didn't begrudge Roach whatever they'd had either, especially since he'd obviously cared about her.

What struck her most about it all was that the exact same thing that had been driving Roach to wage this war was also driving Ash. Not just the concept of seeking vengeance, but vengeance sought for the exact same person.

Jess Sweeney.

Given this unexpected kinship with the chief, Ash felt determined to somehow find him on the surface of Eresos, and to reunite with him. More than ever, she wanted to work with Roach to defeat the Quatro, even if he didn't want to work with Oneiri Team any longer.

"Sweeney." It was Captain Black, subvocalizing so that she heard him over her implant.

"Yes, Captain?"

"The Quatro and their new mechs have reached Ingress, and they're digging again. This time, they seem much likelier to succeed. They've started their tunnel out of range of the city walls, on top of a hill. Those mechs of theirs seem to be even more proficient diggers than the Quatro themselves. They also have Red Company with them, helping them to defend the tunnel mouth."

"Does that mean what I think it means, sir?"

"If you think it means that your pilots need to get into their mechs right away, to jump down to the surface ahead of the elevator, then yes. Yes, it does."

CHAPTER 42

Nature's Original Shape

If Wound had ever doubted that his new battle suit was built by the same species that built the Gatherers, after seeing how quickly the suits enabled Quatro to tunnel through the earth, he doubted no longer.

He knew that the walls of the city the humans called Ingress extended below the planet's surface for nearly two hundred meters, but that did not faze him. His great paws could morph to become wide, flat surfaces, ideal for displacing great mounds of dirt, and the front of the battle suit could change to fit the tunnel's dimensions, plowing the piles of earth back to the surface.

Whenever Wound encountered rock, he simply blasted it apart and transported the pieces out of the tunnel.

He didn't relish this task, nor did he look forward to the lives he knew he would have to take once he and the others infiltrated the city.

Or do I? Because it is true that I dream at night of ripping out human jugulars with my teeth, of watching the scarlet spurt and letting it coat my face before I drink deeply of that—

Wound shook his head savagely. That thought had *not* been his own.

The voices the battle suit seemed to produce had grown loud enough for him to understand their words almost every time they whispered to him, now. Often, they paraded as his own thoughts, and once—just once—he'd found himself believing it.

That had scared him. He'd opened up the suit on that night and fled from it, running through field and forest to try to escape the voices, which did not follow him outside the mech.

After he'd returned, the suit had accepted him willingly once more, and the voices had abated for a time.

But now that he needed to be inside the suit for a prolonged period, it seemed they had come back, stronger than before.

"We'll let this planet burn," Wound muttered as he emerged from the tunnel with a load of earth, depositing it on the mound that had been building steadily for over two hours.

"What did you say?" Saul turned toward him, studying Wound from within the stolen MIMAS mech, which he piloted now.

"What?" Wound said, trying to keep his voice from coming out too loudly, which could easily happen while inside the suit. "I said nothing."

"You did. You said something about letting Eresos burn."

"Well, chaos is nature's original shape. It's best for us to accept that, immerse ourselves in it, and aid in its spread. We will weather entropy far better if we become its agents."

Saul's MIMAS was very still.

Slowly, Wound registered what had just happened. "S-Saul, I did not say that. It was the suit. That was not my sentiment."

"Uh huh. You're going to need to keep it together for us, Wound. We need you shipshape, if we're going to pull this off. Darkstream's going to send everything it has against us. You know that, right?"

"I do. I...should return to digging."

"You do that."

"Do you...do you think they have her inside the city walls?"

"Her? Who's her?"

"My mate. I lost her, long ago. She came to me in a dream last night. I believe she may be within."

"Wound—"

But Wound turned, stalking back inside the tunnel that crept toward the city of Ingress, inch by inch. His work, mostly. The other Quatro, with whom he'd always been so close...he wondered why, now. What did they offer him that rightly compensated him for his contributions?

Nothing.

Always prying where they weren't welcome, were the Quatro. All of them. His entire species. With sanctimonious words of solidarity and community, they sought to control each other. To control *him.* Wasn't freedom the reason they'd left the Home Systems in the first place? And now they'd come to this!

They deserve everything they've gotten.

Wound had often wondered whether the price they'd paid in coming here, in freeing themselves from the Assembly of Elders, had been worth it.

He didn't wonder that anymore.

It was worth it, all right. Well worth it. Because now I have found true freedom, inside a community worthy of me.

This disjointed line of thought continued for some time, the whispers encouraging him all the while, urging him on.

Eventually, they fell silent, and Wound paused digging, raising his head from his work, having been struck by the faint notion that something had just happened to him.

CHAPTER 43

Our Best Idea

Ash's parachute disengaged, fluttering away into the sky, and she plummeted the rest of the way, heavy metal feet hitting the earth with incredible force, all of which was absorbed by her mech's complex system of shocks.

All around her, Oneiri Team came crashing down, and even inside her own mech—even inside the dream—she could feel the tremors their impacts caused.

"Let's move," Ash said over the team-wide as Richaud, the last to land, touched down.

The five of them sprinted over the grassy terrain, toward where the quads were digging their tunnel on a hilltop.

"This doesn't seem like our best idea," Marco said as they ran, his voice carrying none of the strain it should have, traveling with such speed. That was the beauty of piloting a **MIMAS**. "We're attacking mechs we know to be superior to ours. Those mechs outnumber us, and we know them to be supported by a lot of Quatro as well as Red Company mercenaries. Not only that, the terrain favors them, not us. Our odds suck, Steam."

The dream-sky flashed bright orange with Ash's annoyance. "I think your nickname will be Spirit, Marco. Because you're clearly so good at raising ours." She was sure it was a bad idea to christen Marco with his nickname out of sarcasm, and the others might not even accept it. "We have no choice but to engage. If we don't, they'll be inside Ingress in short order. It's why we jumped down in the first place."

No answer from Marco. Maybe he was mulling over the nickname she'd given him.

Red Company fighters were distributed around the hill's slope, and they began firing on the MIMAS mechs the moment they were in range—with sniper fire first, followed quickly by rockets, mortars, and grenades.

The ground Oneiri Team ran on quickly became a warzone, peppered by explosions.

"Don't just count on your mech to endure these, people," Ash barked over the team-wide. "We don't know how many hits like that we can take, and we all saw how banged up Chief Roach's mech was when he came back, so we know we're far from invincible."

The others did as she told them, weaving left and right, slowing at random intervals and speeding at others. In this way, they made it as difficult as possible for the mercenaries to score a direct hit on their mechs.

Even so, a rocket caught Henrietta full in the chest, knocking her MIMAS back, though she caught herself with her left hand, propelling herself straight back into a run.

Shortly after, Richaud failed to anticipate a grenade's trajectory, and it exploded near him, washing his mech with flame and leaving it singed.

Still, Oneiri Team barreled on.

And then they were at the hillside. As they bounded up the slope, Ash opted for her heavy machine gun, picking off Red Company fighters one by one.

Richaud favored a slightly less subtle approach, running and gunning with both rotary autocannons firing at full bore. Beth started out launching grenades, but soon switched to her own machine gun after the second bomb rolled down the hill to explode harmlessly, far from any target. Marco and Henrietta switched between their heavy machine guns interspersed with occasional rockets, to target areas where the enemy were clustered together.

No one used their lasers, since it would have been a waste to use up that much energy on mere infantry.

Either way, in short order, the Red Company mercenaries were sent into full flight, running as fast as they could toward the sanctuary of the hilltop.

Ash stowed her heavy machine gun and caught up with two of the mercenaries, a man and a woman. Extending both bayonets, she took them both in their backs with the blades.

Suddenly, she drew to a stop on the steep slope. It struck her that those were the first human beings she'd killed...well, ever. Before, all her targets had been aliens, which had seemed more acceptable, somehow, especially since she kept her sister's death at the front of her mind at all times.

The sky flashed a dark green—the color of nausea, she quickly realized.

"Steam?" Richaud said, turning toward her from a position farther up on the hill. "You all right?"

"Yeah," Ash said, shaking herself, then continuing up the hill.

Without warning, three quads leapt into view. One of them charged straight at Ash.

She ripped the heavy machine gun from her back once more, opening fire. The quad seemed to simply absorb the bullets, though her implant did track flecks of shrapnel flying off the enemy mech with each impact.

Then, the Quatro mech reached her, running her over, sending her tumbling backward down the hill, the machine gun flying from her grasp and cartwheeling on ahead of her.

She scrambled to find her footing as the world rotated around her again and again. At last, she regained her feet, looking around desperately for her foe.

There. Coming straight at her, again, on a diagonal across the hillside.

Ash leapt into the air, retracting her hands against her wrists and opening fire with the autocannons they revealed, pelting the quad with round after armor-piercing round.

The Quatro mech seemed to snarl up at her, and its back morphed to form what appeared to be a giant cannon. The cannon produced a savage blast of energy, which connected with Ash's mech in midair, causing her to flip over and over until she collided with the ground.

"Retreat," she rasped, the pain almost too great for her to speak. "Fall back, now. We need to wait for the others."

She found her footing again, and then she sprinted toward Ingress, barely checking to see whether the other mechs were following.

Some leader you turned out to be.

Her heavy machine gun still lay somewhere on the hillside, she realized.

It's gone.

CHAPTER 44

Training

Lisa's militia made their way through the streets with as much speed as they could manage, though she'd trained them well enough that they stayed methodical, checking and double-checking blind spots as well as anywhere an enemy could be hiding. The places they couldn't check, such as the balconies that occasionally overhung Habitat 2's streets, they remained constantly vigilant of.

They encountered a Darkstream squad, and Lisa's people didn't hesitate. They didn't glance at her for confirmation, and they certainly didn't ask her over the militia-wide channel for permission to engage.

Instead, they met the perplexed expressions of the Darkstream soldiers by raising their firearms to sight briefly down the barrels and opening fire.

The entire squad of Darkstream soldiers went down without firing a single shot.

Lisa could scarcely believe it. *The sight of a group of civilians out in the streets must have confused them. They didn't consid-*

er us a threat. Highly unlikely we'll get that kind of advantage again. But still...

Trained Darkstream soldiers should not have taken for granted that the people of Habitat 2 would be toothless.

Lisa flashed back to the confines of the beetle as she, Andy, and Tessa traveled across the wilderness of Alex, back when Tessa had first called Lisa out for...well, for being useless, due to totally inadequate Darkstream training.

Tessa had accused the company of relying too heavily on lucid for training their soldiers, and she'd called lucid unsuited to the purpose anyway, without the presence of an experienced trainer who could calibrate a trainee's implant so that each lucid simulation accurately reflected her actual abilities.

Over the months that followed, Tessa had proved herself right, simply by helping Lisa to improve drastically under her tutelage.

Lisa forced herself back to the present. "Stay sharp," she said over the wide channel. "Don't get cocky just because we swept one engagement. The next group we meet will shoot back. I can guarantee that."

But they got lucky, and they didn't encounter either Darkstream or Daybreak operatives on their way to the beetle bay.

Not so, inside the bay itself. Lisa's M-level clearance still gave her access to almost every security feed in the city, and she patched the view of the vehicle bay through to her soldiers' implants.

Another memory: this one from *before* being cooped up inside the beetle with Andy and Tessa. She flashed back to the three of them creeping through Habitat 2, doing their best to avoid the fighting that still raged on between Daybreak and Darkstream.

They'd reached their destination: a different beetle bay from the one Lisa and her militia would attack today. Tessa had told her to wait outside while she went in and dealt with the trio of Daybreak goons inside.

Things were different, today. This time, there were a dozen Darkstream soldiers inside the vehicle bay, and when her militia detonated the breaching charge, blowing open the door, it was Lisa that tossed a flashbang and then followed it inside.

The flashbang appeared to have disoriented most of the twelve soldiers, but three of them must have spotted it in time to take action to mitigate its effects.

Whatever they'd done, they were prepared to fire on Lisa soon after she entered, and in response, she ran for the nearest beetle while her people poured into the bay after her. Both Lisa and the next two soldiers executed covering fire that saw her safely to the protection of the vehicle.

She didn't stop there—that's what they would have expected. Instead, she circled around the vehicle, finding one disoriented Darkstream operative behind it and dispatching her with a point-blank bullet to the temple.

Next, she encountered a man just recovering from the flashbang's effects, who was back-on to her.

Lisa didn't hesitate, squeezing the trigger with her muzzle pointed at the back of his neck. He crumpled to the floor.

"Clear." It was Tessa, subvocalizing across the militia-wide channel.

That meant they needed Lisa back near the entrance, where the controls were located for the airlock, which was built big enough to allow the passage of the bulky beetles.

Once Lisa reached the controls, she used her biometrics to open the outer door, while keeping an eye on the vid feed that showed the airlock's interior.

A few seconds later, she closed the outer door, repressurized the airlock, and opened the wide portal that led into the beetle bay.

Rug entered, wearing her form-fitting blue pressure suit, with two energy weapons affixed to the shoulders. Flanking her were four other Quatro—two on each side.

Lisa smiled down on them. "It's good to see you," she called. Then she closed the inner door, depressurized the airlock, and opened the outer door for the next five aliens to enter.

CHAPTER 45

A Monster or a Coward

Across the plains, Gabe saw Oneiri Team rushing foolishly to engage the force on the hilltop, comprised of Red Company fighters, Quatro, and quads.

He'd been toying with the idea of establishing contact with the descending space elevator. He knew Darkstream would have sent a reserve battalion to deal with the deteriorating situation on Eresos, and he assumed whoever was in command of it would be there, enjoying a leisurely ride down while the **MIMAS** mechs struggled against impossible odds below.

But Oneiri's mad rush at the enemy left no time for chitchat.

Or does it?

Keeping his distance from the enemy for as long as he could, Gabe circled the hill at a wide remove, running at full speed, until he judged he was directly opposite Oneiri's angle of attack.

Around the time he figured they'd made contact with the enemy, he rushed up the hill as quickly as he could.

It was just as he'd expected. The mercenaries had arrayed themselves to confront the Darkstream mechs, leaving just the Quatro on the hilltop to guard the tunnel mouth.

He peered at them with as little of himself exposed as possible, his alien mech changing color to match the terrain, a camouflaging function that he hadn't anticipated. Then again, he hadn't anticipated much of anything about this mech.

He conducted everything through the dream, now—he dreamed his entire life, a process he knew was facilitated by his implant. But he no longer had access to its interface.

Instead, he simply willed what he wanted it to do, and it happened. At present, he wanted to speak to the commander of the reserve force aboard that space elevator, and Captain Arkady Black appeared before him.

Even now, the fact that the captain stood in full view of the enemy made Gabe's throat tighten, until he recalled that Black was visible only to him.

"So, you're the one they slated to command this fool's errand," Gabe said.

With that, he left his cover, willing his arms to become massive energy cannons, both which began to pelt the unclad Quatro with truncated bolts of light. The force of the massless ordnance blasted the aliens off of their feet, one by one.

Arkady Black ran beside Gabe, easily keeping pace, inside the dream. "What is it you want, Roach? I'm only humoring you because I have basically nothing to do aboard this elevator. I'm given to understand you've gone postal."

You have the fight of your life ahead of you, and you have nothing to do? "When we spoke at Plenitos, you told me I was headed for a fall. Well, it's here, Black—for both of us."

Soon after neutralizing his fifth Quatro, Gabe succeeded in getting the attention of one of the quads. It rushed out of the tunnel mouth, barreling toward him, eyes aglow, shoulders shifting and morphing to prepare something nasty for him.

Gabe flung himself forward, his own mech shifting radically, gathering together to form a great wheel with serrated edges. The wheel he had become landed just before the alien, spinning straight over it, laying it open down the middle. Gabe's edge almost sheared through to the Quatro inside the quad, but it twisted aside at the last second, metal whirling and transforming to enable the maneuver.

Instantly, Gabe's wheel resumed a humanoid form, and he caught himself on the ground, kneeling, aiming a massive gun that took shape as he steadied it on his other arm.

This time, a single cannonball emerged, knocking the quad clean off the hilltop and down to the slope below.

"Be more specific, Roach," Black said from beside him. "What do you mean by a fall?"

Gabe turned to confront the next quad, flattening himself close to the ground to avoid an energy blast it had sent his way.

"Do you have fuel air explosives on that elevator?"

Black glanced at Gabe sharply. "Fuel air explosives are not authorized for use on—"

Gabe sprang several meters into the air, over the charging quad, and fired parts of himself at his foe at high speed. A jagged spear skewered the quad, pinning it to the ground, and the moment Gabe landed, he sprinted toward his immobilized foe.

The Quatro managed to free itself by the time Gabe neared, bounding away to the left. Gabe summoned the parts of himself he'd used for ordnance, and it walked, flipped, and rolled toward him. When the fragments reached him, they rejoined him, and they became one once more.

"I didn't ask whether you're authorized to use them, Black," Gabe snarled. "I asked whether you have them with you, and I don't know why I bothered, because I already know that you do. I've been around long enough, I'm well-connected enough, to know that major Darkstream missions *always* have fuel air bombs on hand, and it insults my intelligence for you to suggest otherwise."

Four other quads had just appeared from the mouth of the tunnel, and they now were attempting to surround Gabe.

He turned and fled down the hillside. Inside the dream, Black also fled, running without exertion.

"The Quatro command the high ground," Gabe said as he ran. "We can't afford to engage them there, and so we have to summon them elsewhere. To do that, we'll attack what they must defend: the tunnel. You need to dig down to it and fill it with every fuel air explosive you have. If you fail to do that, the city will be lost."

"We aren't authorized to use fuel air explosives, Roach."

"Are you authorized to lose Ingress? I told you, Black. The fall is here, and you need to choose, between defeat and disgrace. I'm leading these quads from their hilltop, for as long as they'll follow me. That will lessen the pressure enough for you to do what needs to be done. I only have to look at the elevator to see you've almost arrived on the surface. The timing works out, as long as you don't squander the opportunity I've given you." As he ran, Gabe turned to lock eyes with Black. "The question you have to ask yourself is whether you want history to view you as a monster or a coward."

Gabe evicted Black from the dream, then. He was tired of looking at him, and he'd already done what he could to try to persuade the man. If only simpering would convince him, then he would not be convinced, because Gabe did not simper.

CHAPTER 46

Supposed to Be the Best

Jake made liberal use of his **MIMAS'** launch capacity to maneuver around the comet, evading the alien mech's charges as well as its ordnance. He wasn't too concerned about fuel reserves, considering the low gravity meant very little had to be expended to displace himself.

A miscalculation led to getting hit by an energy blast from his enemy, causing him to flip away into space, his stomach a hard knot of pain.

Finally, he managed to stabilize and rocket back toward the comet. But the alien mech hadn't wasted time positioning itself for Jake's return. The moment he landed, it drove its hand, which had morphed to form a spike, into Jake's chest.

Kicking out swiftly with his left foot, Jake used it to boost away in order to minimize the impact of the mech's blow. To avoid getting impaled.

The maneuver resulted in his feet leaving the comet once more, and he just accepted that, putting more distance between him and his enemy by opening fire with both rotary autocannons.

The alien mech leapt at him, but this time, a Banshee missile from the *Javelin* rocketed into it, shunting it aside and detonating. It was the mech's turn to flip end over end through space, its side blasted open, though when Jake zoomed in he saw that it was repairing itself rapidly.

In the dream, Captain Bronson appeared on the comet's surface, glaring up at Jake. "I thought you were supposed to be the best!" he barked.

"Uh…well, if you look at my lucid scores—"

"I don't care about your lucid scores. Right now, I need you to get these things off of my destroyer! I've already told Engineering to reprogram the point defense turrets so that they don't shoot down your ordnance."

"Yes, sir."

"Bronson out."

The captain vanished, and Jake used his launch thrusters to put the comet between himself and the alien mech. That done, he spun around while suspended in space, so that he faced the *Javelin* and the machines that crawled all over it, ripping up its hull.

The **MIMAS** augmented its user's vision dramatically, and Jake used that now to zoom in on the ship and draw a bead on one of the little metal critters.

He fired a rocket, which screamed across the black expanse between him and the destroyer.

His target skittered aside, and the rocket hit the destroyer's hull, tearing a gaping hole in her. The explosion seared the enemy robot, too, but it seemed no worse for wear.

"No rockets," Bronson yelled, reappearing right beside Jake, the agitation in his voice mounting. "They're not a good idea even if they *do* hit!"

"Sorry, sir," Jake choked out.

He reached behind his back to detach his heavy machine gun, swinging it around and zooming in to target the next robot.

The alien mech collided with him from behind, sending the heavy machine gun flying away through space.

Jake struggled to turn in the thing's iron grip, with no success. Then, he remembered a trick he'd used during his first encounter with the Quatro. He let a grenade roll out of his launcher, without actually launching it.

It exploded, and waves of agony crashed over Jake. But it seemed to take the AI, or whatever was animating the alien mech, by surprise, and its grip loosened enough for Jake to wrench free and rocket toward his heavy machine gun.

He caught it, flipped around, and retargeted the tiny robot he'd aimed for before, which was making its way toward one of the destroyer's main engines.

This time, the robot disintegrated under the machine gun's armor-piercing rounds.

Got one.

The alien mech was coming at him again, and Jake boosted away from it—closer to the destroyer.

He let loose with a healthy helping of rockets, targeting his adversary. The enemy mech managed to evade most of them, but one took it in the center of its chest, the fluid metal surface peeling away, presumably to try to mitigate the damage. A second rocket hit the alien mech full in the face.

"Like that?" Jake said from inside the dream, his success sending a thrill through him.

Something hit him from behind, tearing at the surface of his MIMAS.

One of the robots. *It left the destroyer!*

Jake reached behind him with his right hand, but he couldn't manage to reach the little jerk. Then he tried with his left, catching the thing's ankle and yanking it in front of him where it squirmed to get free, metal claws swiping at Jake's face.

He grabbed the thing's arm with his free hand and ripped it clean in two.

Nuisance. Throwing both halves at the alien mech, he turned to pick off more of the robotic devils.

Jake managed to neutralize three more before turning to find the other mech recovered from his earlier salvo and barreling through the void, straight at him.

The alien mech connected with Jake's MIMAS, sending it backward. Several long seconds later, both mechs crashed into the *Javelin*, and Jake felt the hull buckle beneath him.

CHAPTER 47

Defensive Formation

When they reached Ingress' walls, Oneiri Team met Arkady Black and the rest of the Darkstream battalion emerging from the city, accompanied by what appeared to be an enormous tunnel borer.

When he saw the mechs approach, Black gave a self-satisfied nod. "Over-reliance on those contraptions has sent you away with your tails between your legs again, I see."

The sky flashed red with Ash's anger. "Sir, you're the one who ordered us to jump from the elevator and engage the enemy by ourselves. You should know that the **MIMAS** mechs aren't at their best simply going it alone, unsupported, just as we never deploy a force consisting only of tanks. The mechs work best when working together with a battalion of varied composition."

Black's graying mustache twitched as he returned her stare, his neck craning to meet her mech's gaze.

"You're right," he said at last. "I've let my pride get the better of me, and I'm not offering an analysis that's fair or justified. I apologize."

"Apology accepted, sir."

"Now, a short while ago I spoke with Chief Roach, and—"

"You were in contact with the chief?" Ash exclaimed before she could stop herself.

"That's what I just said. He had a decent idea: start digging down to intercept the enemy's tunnel. It should be fairly straightforward to anticipate the tunnel's trajectory, and we can confirm with step-frequency radar. Once we reach their tunnel, we'll uh...fill it with fuel air explosives."

Ash paused as she digested the last few words Black had spoken, which he'd practically mumbled. "Wait—fuel air bombs? We're not authorized to use those on Eresos!"

"We...actually are, if it's deemed necessary. We have them on hand at all times, in case the necessity arises. It's not a fact we publicize, but it's true. This was Roach's idea, Sweeney. Anyway, it's possible we won't have to use them. Once the enemy spots what we're doing, there's a good chance they'll come off the high ground to attack us, right where we want them to."

For a long moment, Ash tried to digest what Black had told her. The thought of getting out of her mech, breaking her contract with Darkstream, and facing the consequences crossed her mind.

This is wrong. Ash had heard whispers of fuel air bombs being used against the Quatro during the first clashes between them and humanity, and that was bad enough. But the idea of returning to their use, despite years of a universal agreement that doing so was immoral...

The only thing that stopped her from objecting was the fact that Roach had been the one to suggest it. Roach, who shared her motivation for participating in this war.

Maybe the Quatro truly do deserve this.

"Okay," she said haltingly. "Let's do it, then."

Black had been watching her body language closely—there wasn't much else to watch while she was inside her MIMAS, in terms of gauging her reaction—and now he gave a curt nod, turning to face the rest of the reserve battalion he commanded.

"Move *out*, people!"

They did, rolling across the hills in formation, with a tank on each side, infantry in front, and two personnel carriers in the center, flanking the tunnel borer.

They soon reached their destination: a shallow rise, fairly close to the city, and out of firing range of the hill occupied by the Quatro and Red Company.

"We know the composition of the ground surrounding Ingress, and we know that our boring machine can dig at a rate of ten meters an hour, here. The borer is basically cutting-edge when it comes to digging holes, and if we assume the Quatro can dig at roughly the same speed, then there's a good chance our tunnel will intercept theirs before it's finished, especially since they have to tunnel upward after digging down two hundred meters to clear the walls."

"A good chance?" Ash said. "We're basing our entire strategy on a 'good chance' it will work?"

"That's all any strategy is ever based on," Black retorted, loud enough for those around them to hear. "The alternative is attacking the enemy at their superior position and getting crushed. Chief Roach is currently in the process of leading four of the enemy quads as far away as he can, so the enemy's progress should be impeded for a time, anyway. I'll thank you to stop questioning my orders, now, Sweeney. This works best if we're all united."

"Yes, sir," Ash said, and she meant it. They were committed to this course, now, and she agreed that it didn't serve anything to continue debating things with her superior.

They set the boring machine to digging. In less than an hour, it had dug its length through the ground. They could still see it, though—its butt end was right there, pointing at them at an angle.

The process seemed excruciatingly slow. *Can this really work?*

But it did work. As Black had said, they didn't actually need to intercept the enemy tunnel. They only needed to convince the enemy that they *could* intercept it.

The enemy was soon convinced, and a force left the hilltop consisting of two platoons' worth of mercenaries, three dozen Quatro...and one quad, its eyes glowing even in the daylight.

Then, having zoomed in on the enemy force, Ash saw it: in the midst of the mercenaries was Tommy's mech, striding forward, hands already retracted to reveal twin rotary autocannons.

Bastards.

"Get ready, people," Black barked. "That quad is still just as mighty as it was before. We're merely facing it on terrain where we're not *guaranteed* to get slaughtered." He turned, sweeping his eyes over his forces. "Defensive formation!"

CHAPTER 48

The Long-Term
Doesn't Matter

Bronson gripped the Captain's chair armrests until his knuckles were white and his hands shook.

When the alien mech had managed to drive Price into the side of the destroyer, and his sensor operator reported they'd nearly punctured the hull, that had made his heart rate spike. The idea of two giant mechs inside his ship, tearing apart her guts with their fighting, did not help him to relax.

Then, Price had managed to get the enemy mech away from the destroyer once more, back toward the comet. But the thing was delivering a beating to the boy, knocking him all around both ice and space, periodically hitting him with ordnance that sent him spinning wildly within the low gravity.

In the meantime, the little robots continued to ravage the *Javelin*'s hull. Several of them had broken through, and Bronson had squads of marines roaming the corridors, engaging them whenever they found the things. It was imperative that his soldiers stop the robots before they managed to access vital systems and tear them apart.

The things fought almost as well as they perforated destroyer hulls, however, and Bronson had already lost three people.

The worst part of all this was his total inability to *do* anything about it.

The alien mech had quickly grown proficient at anticipating and avoiding the destroyer's heavier ordnance. If they could actually land a few more hits, this engagement would be going differently, but the thing was smart, and fast.

"Try kinetic impactors again, Tactical," Bronson barked. "This time, execute a two hundred meter spread, along a line that cuts across the alien mech's likely trajectory. Without hitting Price!"

"Yes, sir."

Seconds later, the shot was off, the rounds speeding across the void toward the shape-shifting machine.

But it had anticipated the volley once more, and it rocketed aside, the kinetic impactors screaming harmlessly into space.

"*Damn* it," Bronson spat. "Sensor operator, show me a zoomed-in visual of both mechs fighting again."

Soon, the main viewscreen once again showed the giant robots locked in combat—exchanging rockets and armor-piercing rounds, charging each other in turn, and maneuvering through space using their launch thrusters.

It's not just that the alien mech is stronger. Price has lost his spirit.

The boy's head simply wasn't in the game anymore, and it had happened when the alien mech had knocked him into the destroyer's hull. For whatever reason, that had screwed with his mindset, and he didn't seem likely to regain it, barring something drastic.

That gave Bronson an idea. He didn't feel confident it was a great idea. In fact, he was pretty sure the long-term consequences would be bad.

The long-term doesn't matter if we lose in the short-term.

He had no other option. And so, with the help of Engineering as well as the *Javelin*'s most advanced AIs, he began transmitting instructions to Price's implant, without Price ever being notified that it was happening.

God help him. God help me, after Price realizes what I've done.

There was nothing for it. As always, Bronson did what survival demanded.

It wasn't in him to do otherwise.

CHAPTER 49

Lay Down Your Guns

They admitted Rug and the other Quatro into the beetle bay without incident, and then the combined forces of Lisa's militia and Rug's people filed into the streets of Habitat 2 to begin progressing toward the freight elevator that would take them to the roof.

They moved in two groups, separated by two streets at all times—the Quatro in one and Lisa's militia in the other, with the exception of Andy, who was helping the aliens to navigate the city streets.

Five blocks away from the beetle bay, they turned a corner to find an entire platoon of Darkstream soldiers, stretched across the street, with Commander Mario Laudano at their head. They'd erected temporary barricades to take cover behind.

They must have been watching us on the security feeds. Anticipated our trajectory.

"Going somewhere, Seaman Sato?" Laudano called down the street to her.

Before answering, she subvocalized to Andy: "Have you encountered any resistance?"

"Negative."

"We have. A whole platoon of Darkstream soldiers, led by Laudano. Do you have a viable route to flank?"

A pause, then: "Yes, ma'am. We can cut through a couple alleyways then come at them from behind."

"Do it. But be careful. Judging by the barricades they've thrown up, they knew we were coming, which seems to suggest they know about the Quatro, too."

"Giving me the silent treatment today, Sato?" Laudano said. "I can simply order my people to mow yours down, if you like."

Lisa might have ordered her people to retreat, but that would have led to a confused mess, probably with discrete firefights occurring across several streets and alleyways. It also likely would have meant Laudano shooting some of her people in their backs.

That's no way for them to die. If they have to go down today, they'll go down staring the company that betrayed them straight in the eye.

"You're with Daybreak," Lisa said, proud that her voice didn't waver as it rang out, though it reverberated against the nearby structures.

"Yes," Laudano said.

A brief silence followed.

"Did you expect me to deny it?" the commander continued. "Because there's no point in my doing so. The outcome will be the same whether I confess it or not. You're outnumbered, Sato. Even supposing your amateurs manage to defeat my force of professional soldiers—a laughable prospect, but I'll humor you—it doesn't matter. The rest of my people are helping Daybreak to lock down the city as we speak, and together they outnumber you four-to-one. This ends with you defeated and enslaved, with no system net access and no chance of rescue. Why not lay down your guns now and surrender? If you do that, I'll see what *I* can do about keeping the worst of Cooper's beasts away from you."

"We'll take our chances," Lisa said, sighting down her assault rifle at Laudano's head and firing a burst.

He was already making for the barricades, however, and his people had begun firing on Lisa's, who made for what scant cover there was: a single alley, four doorways. Many of them simply huddled against the sides of the buildings themselves.

Maybe I made the wrong call in not retreating.

She saw two of her militia make for the same doorway at once, resulting in them both getting mowed down, their bodies spasming on the way to the ground.

Lisa managed to make it to the alley, and she unclipped a grenade from her belt, pulling out the pin with her teeth and then lobbing the explosive at the enemy.

It went off on the wrong side of the barricades, causing the Darkstream soldiers to duck momentarily, but doing no real damage.

"Andy, how close are you?" she subvocalized.

"Getting there, ma'am. Sit tight."

She felt her lips curl into a tight smile. Probably, she should have told Andy to stop calling her ma'am a while ago, but she enjoyed hearing him say it too much for that.

Popping out of the alleyway again, she fired at the first target she saw, and this time she was rewarded by a Darkstream soldier's face acquiring some new holes. Blood flew, and he fell backward onto Habitat 2's simulated cobble.

"We're here," Andy said.

"Good. Hit them!"

The rumble of the Quatro's approach should have been audible to the Darkstream soldiers—hell, they should have felt the street vibrating through their boots, if nothing else. But none of them turned to face the Quatro. They just continued to fire on Lisa's militia.

Seconds later, Lisa learned why. Soldiers appeared on four separate balconies, eight of them in total, all bearing rocket launchers.

They fired on the massive aliens before withdrawing into their respective buildings. A firestorm blossomed in the streets of Habitat 2, well beyond Laudano's fighters.

"No!" Lisa cried, her voice coming out strangled and raw. "Forward! Forward!"

She knew the impulse bordered on suicidal, but that was Rug and Andy over there, not to mention the rest of the Quatro, who had taken her into their subterranean spaceship and accepted her as one of their own.

Lisa ran to the doorway that two of her soldiers had tried for before, taking it herself, firing around it at Laudano and his killers.

"Andy!" she screamed, not bothering to subvocalize. "Andy?" Her insides felt like ice, and a cold sweat broke out across her forehead.

No answer. "Rug?" she yelled. Nothing.

She ripped another grenade from her belt, and this time she managed to get it behind the barricades. The Darkstream soldiers scattered, some of them back toward the dissipating rocket explosions, others out past the barricades, toward Lisa.

She didn't squander the opportunity. Instead, she took aim, felling the nearest Darkstream operative, then smoothly switching targets to another.

Everything Tessa had taught her guided her now, the instincts her friend had instilled enabling her to deal cold death to the enemy.

Tessa herself drew up beside Lisa, but they did not look at each other. Instead, they marched forward in lockstep, taking down everything before them that moved.

The rocket launchers appeared on the balconies once more, and Lisa switched to targeting them. "Shoot the soldiers on the balconies!" she screamed over her militia-wide.

Sniper fire took out two of them—that would be Phineas Gage and Bob O'Toole, from the rear of the militia's formation, not that it could really be called that anymore.

Five of the soldiers with rocket launchers went down in rapid succession...six...and then the remaining two loosed rockets straight at Lisa's snipers.

The final pair of balcony targets went down to her and Tessa's bullets, but when Lisa tried to raise Phineas and O'Toole on the militia-wide, she got no response.

Her fear had turned to rage, and now her veins ran hot with molten fire. She found herself stepping through the barricades, checking them one by one for enemies that remained.

Behind the third, she found Laudano. He sprang up at her, combat knife in hand—he must have lost his gun in the panic after she'd thrown the grenade.

Lisa put a round in his forehead, and that was that.

As suddenly as it had started, the fight was over.

"Andy," she breathed, rushing forward, searching through the thinning smoke.

If it hadn't been for subvocalization, she never would have heard him call her name, his reconstructed voice sounding flat, detached.

Seconds after he spoke, she located him, huddled against a building, face covered in streams of red. One of his legs ended at the knee, and the other was a mess of flesh, fabric, and blood.

She bent down, wrapped her arms around him, and stood up, straining with his weight. "Oh, Andy," she said, taking a step forward in search of her other friends.

Many of them, she found sprawled across the street, inert.

"Check them," she called to the others of her militia. "See whether they're still alive. Check every one."

"Lisa," Tessa said.

She turned, Andy's weight pulling her arms downward. Gravity fought to take him from her.

"*What?*" she spat.

"We have to go," Tessa said. "Right now. If we don't, none of us will get to leave. We have no way to transport these Quatro, even if some of them do still live."

"Where's Phineas Gage? Bob O'Toole?"

"O'Toole made it to cover. The rockets got Gage."

Lisa's throat clenched, and tears stung her eyes. She staggered down the street as the smoke continued to clear, her militia at her back.

Large forms loomed ahead, resolving into Quatro. Rug was at their front—limping badly, but still alive.

Handing Andy to Tessa, Lisa ran toward her. The Quatro lowered her head, and Lisa wrapped her arms around the alien.

"Rug."

"Lisa," the Quatro said, panting. Her breathing sounded labored.

"We have to go."

They pressed on together, toward the freight elevator. Of the original forty-two, there were nineteen Quatro left standing, and Lisa's militia numbered only nine, now. Everyone else, they'd left for dead on the streets of Habitat 2.

There's nothing we could do, she told herself. But she knew that today would rob her sleep for a long time to come.

When the doors opened onto Habitat 2's rooftop—to the waning sun, which cast red rays sideways across the metal—they found Darkstream's ten shuttles prepped and ready to go.

Laudano had them all prepared, so that they could leave the moment Habitat 2 was safely in Daybreak's hands.

Lisa's security clearance still worked, and she used it to open the airlock of the nearest shuttle before the pilot could react.

Once inside, she made her way to the cockpit, where the pilot was rising from his seat, his pistol in hand.

He began to raise it, but Lisa was faster. She stepped toward him and placed the barrel of her assault rifle against his forehead.

"You're taking us off this planet," she said. "Radio the other pilots and tell them their shuttles will be destroyed with them inside unless they cooperate fully. And drop that pistol, for God's sake, before I paint this cockpit with your brain."

In short order, the remnants of her militia and the Quatro were all inside the shuttles. Lisa shared a craft with Tessa, Rug, and Andy, along with two other Quatro.

They had no choice but to strap Andy into a crash seat for the takeoff, where Lisa planned to minister to him as best she knew how.

As for the Quatro, they could only lie on the floor and hope their weight would protect them from the rigors of attaining orbit. Lisa thought that it should protect them, but there was nothing more that could be done, at any rate.

"What about the others inside Habitat 2?" Andy croaked. "They'll be slaves, now."

Lisa couldn't believe he was still conscious. "We'll come back for them," she said. "As soon as we can."

Though she lay on the shuttle's deck, Rug's head was still level with Lisa's. It swung toward her. "Where are we going?" she asked.

"To Eresos, Rug. You're about to be reunited with your people."

CHAPTER 50

Payload

Jake was beginning to appreciate how Chief Roach had felt during his battle with the quad.

The alien mech had almost total control over the engagement. It was everything Jake could do to evade its ordnance, and the act of trying to divide up his own shooting between his adversary and the robots attacking the *Javelin* resulted in doing very little damage to either.

He tried keeping the alien mech at bay with his right rotary autocannon while using his implant to zoom in on the robots attacking the *Javelin* and firing at them with his left.

That worked to neutralize two more of the robots, until his inability to split his attention resulted in the alien mech getting the better of him by rocketing to Jake's right to come at him with a hammerhand that had a lot of extra mass, drawn forward from the mech's forearms and biceps.

Jake went spinning out of control from the blow, much faster than he had before, and instead of following him, the mech took a different tack.

It spun around and started to help the smaller robots by pelting the destroyer with ordnance that resembled large, medieval-era cannonballs. The robots had disabled many of the *Javelin*'s point defense turrets, and most of the shots got through.

As Jake stabilized at last, he watched as one of the *Javelin*'s main engines exploded.

No!

Apparently, the mech had figured out that if it neutralized the destroyer, then Jake, Bronson, and the crew of the *Javelin* would be stranded, and the robot army would be able to pick them apart at their leisure.

At least, it certainly looks like it figured that out.

Of course, Jake was the true lynch pin of his and Bronson's defense. Without him, there was simply no way to deal with the robots crawling all over the warship, intent on ripping it apart.

He was their key to victory. And he was failing utterly. Again.

Rocketing at the alien mech, he turned his thrusters' propulsion up to maximum for the first time since they'd started fighting. Before, he'd been too afraid of missing his mark and careening into space, spending precious seconds reorienting himself.

Now, he understood that he simply had to take that risk. The *Javelin* was about to be incapacitated permanently, and when that happened, all would be lost.

As Jake's charge neared his adversary, the alien mech formed a giant metal fist, this time with its right hand only. Then it performed a complex rocketing maneuver that had it swinging around, its fist connecting with Jake just as he was about to collide with it.

As fast as Jake had been coming at the mech, he now traveled that fast away from it, toward the comet, his attempts to make adjustments with his thrusters only increasing his wild spinning. Several agonizing seconds later, he crashed into the comet's surface.

He groaned, and a dark haze descended over everything he could see, which he interpreted as the dream communicating to him that he was nearing the end of his resolve—his will to fight—as well as the end of his energy, his stamina.

Reluctantly, he got to his feet...in time to see the alien mech catch a Banshee missile with cupped hands, swing it around, and reverse its momentum back toward the destroyer, blowing a gaping hole in her side.

With that, the mech did something as unexpected as it was devastating. It turned slowly in midair, toward Jake, but it didn't fire on him—it was as though the mech was trying to tell him something with its cold, inhuman gaze.

Then, it turned toward his father's comet hopper and unloaded a payload of six rockets at it.

Finding strength he didn't know he had, Jake leapt from the comet, using his thrusters to propel himself after the missiles as fast as possible. He took out one of them with his rotary auto-cannons, two of them...but the remaining four reached the *Whale.*

The ship had no chance. It was built for peace, not war—for building, not destruction. It exploded instantly into a million fragments. With his father aboard.

As the world washed with red, Jake turned toward the alien mech, his chin lifting slightly as he glared at the machine that had just taken his father from him.

The afterimage of the *Whale* exploding was still seared into his mind.

Slowly, Jake spread his hands, both bayonets extending. Even though he was in space, where no sound could exist, the dream still rendered the rasp of metal emerging from metal.

He rocketed toward the alien mech.

CHAPTER 51

Dynamo

The Darkstream tanks opened the fight, by pounding away at the enemy as they closed the gap to the hilltop where the tunnel borer was sinking slowly into the earth, seeking the siege tunnel dug by the Quatro.

Judging from the way the quad deftly avoided the anti-tank rounds, the alien piloting it had already grown fairly proficient.

Probably it has some help from the thing's AI, too.

One round clipped its shoulder, then. When it did, the suit seemed to peel away, reforming soon after.

Can these things heal themselves? They reminded Ash of the versatility shown by the Gatherers. When you paired that versatility with a giant war machine piloted by an alien who was deadly even without a mech...

The Darkstream soldiers surged forward several meters, in formation, the front row taking one knee to fire on the approaching mercenaries and Quatro while the row behind them fired over their heads.

A third row remained behind, using the shallow hill to maintain their own firing solution on the enemy.

Red Company had brought rocket launchers, a fact that they'd concealed by hiding the fighters carrying them behind the lumbering Quatro. But now, the aliens peeled away, and rockets flew, with devastating effect on the Darkstream infantry. Ash watched as men and women were blown apart, their limbs spinning through the air to land several meters away.

"Forward, Oneiri Team!" Ash yelled over the team-wide channel. "We can take a lot more punishment than the infantry. We need to start absorbing some of the heat."

Five MIMAS mechs surged past the much smaller soldiers. In response, the three dozen Quatro not in mechs rushed forward, firing on Oneiri with the artillery strapped to their backs.

Oneiri Team answered with a deadly mix of armor-piercing rounds from autocannons, heavy machine gun fire, and grenades fired into the middle of the charging alien ranks. Ash wished she still had her own heavy machine gun, as she valued its increased accuracy, but she made do with her autocannons.

Then the Quatro tide crashed into them, and Oneiri switched to bayonets and flamethrowers.

All around Ash became a confusion of fur and flame and death. She spun wildly, savagely, her bayonet sinking into whatever it could find.

Two Quatro went down, followed by a metal clink, which was followed by a scandalized shout over the team-wide.

"Hey!" It was Richaud. "Watch what you're stabbing with that thing!"

"Sorry," Ash mumbled, the dream world flashing pink with her embarrassment. She turned to find another target.

The Quatro corpses piled up quickly, and Ash allowed herself a measure of satisfaction—until an explosion drew her attention behind her, and she saw what the quad was doing to the rest of the Darkstream force.

It had already succeeded in taking out one of the two tanks, though Ash had not seen how. The noise of its destruction was what had made her look.

The quad made toward the only remaining tank, but to do so, it had to rampage through the humans not inside machines, shooting, impaling, and trampling the Darkstream infantry with alarming efficiency. Once it neutralized the remaining tank, it would no doubt target the tunnel borer.

But Oneiri Team had other matters to attend to. The mercenary piloting Tommy's mech waded through the mounds of Quatro corpses and opened fire with its rotary cannons.

Ash cursed over the team-wide channel. "Spirit, Henrietta, Richaud—you take on the rogue MIMAS. Paste, come with me. We have to deal with that quad."

As they rushed to back up what remained of the Winged Dragons, Beth glanced at her. "Don't you think your allocation of forces is a bit off? I think there should be three of us taking on the quad, at least."

Ash shook her head—she didn't have much time to talk before they reached the quad, but she managed to spit out, "I doubt the mercenary piloting Tommy's mech will even know what to do with that much machine. The others will make short work of it, and you and I can hold off the quad until then."

Then they reached the quad, just as it had started hitting the remaining Darkstream tank with devastating blasts of energy.

Ash sent a rocket its way, and it connected with the Quatro's metal haunches, making it hop forward involuntary, its hind legs lifting off the ground several feet as the explosion blossomed around it.

Then, it turned to charge Ash, and suddenly, remembering how one of these things had knocked Jake down like he'd been a paper soldier, she felt somewhat less sure that she and Beth could keep the thing at bay.

At the last second before the quad tackled her, she sidestepped, coating its flank with a healthy helping of flame.

Extending her right bayonet, she swiped at her enemy, but the quad was too fast. It changed directions, squaring up with Beth to fire on her.

Beth hit the ground, propping herself up with her left hand while firing at the quad with her heavy machine gun, one-handed.

Ash charged the Quatro from behind to drive her bayonets into the alien's haunches, putting her full weight behind the blades. They sunk in several inches, but then the quad turned, swatting at Ash with a single paw and sending her crashing to the ground.

She struggled to get free, but the quad used its other paw to steady her where she lay. As it did, its very head morphed, to form the biggest cannon Ash had ever seen; certainly the biggest one she'd seen the quads' fluid surfaces form.

She could actually see the energy beginning to gather within the barrel, and she felt sure that if it hit her at this range, it would end her. But try as she might, she could not extract herself from beneath the quad's girth.

Something collided with the quad from side on, then—a blur of dark gray followed by a trail of orange, yellow, and red.

It was Henrietta, shunting the quad aside, using her thrusters to do it, just as Ash had out on the Barrens. The quad's head-cannon unleashed its energy less than a foot from Ash's head, putting a giant crater in the ground.

Before the quad could right itself to throw off Henrietta, Ash regained her feet, leapt into the air, and extended her bayonets once more.

While the Quatro was on its side, she dropped, angling her blades toward one of its legs. They drove home, sinking through the metal limb to pin it to the ground below.

Spirit jumped on top of the alien, then, riding it like a mechanical bull. Henrietta remained on top of it, too, helping Ash to keep it in one place.

"Lasers," Ash grunted over the team-wide. "While we have it pinned!"

Richaud and Paste didn't hesitate. They positioned themselves where they wouldn't hit their teammates, and then they trained their new weapons on the quad, dialing the lasers up to full power.

The quad thrashed and twisted beneath them, and one of Ash's bayonets snapped in two. But the other held fast, and she threw her shoulder against the beast as well, to continue holding it in place.

At last, the quad's shifting metal surface twisted, bubbled, and melted through, until the ray of death reached the alien below. The smell of cooking flesh hit Ash, then, along with a piercing wail that seemed to take forever to subside.

"It's done," Beth said.

"Not quite," said Richaud, and something in his voice made Ash turn around.

Two more quads were running at them from the hilltop. They would be here in seconds.

"Get ready, everyone," Ash said, though she didn't feel nearly as confident as she sounded. She still couldn't believe they'd managed to take out one quad—two, though, she felt very little hope of defeating.

Something caught her eye in the distance. She instructed her MIMAS' enhanced vision to zoom in, and when she did, she saw the alien mech from Valhalla station, sprinting across Eresos toward the oncoming Quatro.

Its speed seemed incredible to Ash, and yet the quads did not appear to register its approach. When the enemy mechs were still dozens of meters away, the alien mech—which could only be piloted by Gabriel Roach—crashed into the nearest quad, causing it to skid and tumble across the ground. Gabe traveled with it.

The quad he hadn't targeted broke away from its charge to help its fellow. Twin cannons formed on his shoulders, and Ash recognized the telltale energy buildup.

Gabe thrust both arms toward it, and a jagged spike emerged from each, disrupting the energy and blowing both cannons clean away, twin fragment clouds scattering in the wind.

The quad he'd tackled recovered, standing to come at him, but Gabe turned to meet it, his entire right arm becoming a giant broadsword.

He thrust forward, impaling the quad straight through its neck, and he withdrew the blade just as quickly. That left him ready to react to the other Quatro's charge by leaping into the air, cannons of his own forming to rain down rapid-fire energy on his foe.

The spikes Gabe had used to disable the quad's cannons were now flipping back toward him across the ground, and when he landed, they bounced up to become part of his arms once more.

The quad Gabe had impaled still functioned, somehow. *He must have missed hitting the Quatro inside.*

Both quads charged him together at full gallop, masses gathering on their backs to extend forward and take the shape of lances, which angled toward Gabe's torso. Ash cringed.

The lances struck home, running Gabe through—right in the center, where Ash knew his body had to be.

Gabe's mech went limp, suspended only by the Quatro blades.

Her heart fell.

Most of all, Ash felt saddest for her sister, who'd been killed in cold blood by these animals, and who would have no vengeance, after all.

The quads slowly withdrew their blades, and Gabe slid to the ground.

The moment his face hit the grass, his back morphed, twisting upward to become a massive cannon, which shot one of the quads at point-blank range, causing the front third of it to boil away.

As quickly as it had formed, the cannon disappeared, and Gabe's broadsword was back once again.

He sprang up, driving it forward into the quad's chest, the blade disappearing up to the hilt. When he withdrew it, the alien slumped to the ground. Neither it nor its counterpart moved again.

Slowly, Gabe turned toward Oneiri team, his surface reforming into a humanoid shape.

"How...?" Ash said, then took a deep breath. "How are you still alive?"

Not answering, Gabe walked toward them, until he was just a few meters away, regarding them all silently.

"Where are the other quads?" a voice called, and Ash turned to see Arkady Black, striding between the MIMAS mechs, looking minuscule beside them.

"We fought," Gabe said. "They fled."

Black nodded. "Dynamo," he said, then turned to walk back toward what remained of the Winged Dragons.

"What does that mean?" Ash shouted.

"That should be Roach's nickname," Black said. "Aren't you all coming up with names for each other?"

Ash turned back to Gabe, who stood inert, as though he was part of the landscape. "How are you still alive, Chief?" she asked again. "They impaled you. I saw it. You should be dead."

"I'm not your *chief* any longer. I'm not even human, so I doubt Darkstream will be comfortable with me holding a rank."

"Not...human?"

"My body was starving, inside this thing. Dying of thirst, too. I was still in a coma, Sweeney. This mech can't feed me. It's ridiculous to think it could. It would kill me in the attempt."

"So...what did you do?"

"It offered me a choice. Die, of thirst and starvation, or join with it. Bodily. Dissolve until we became one, its nerves my nerves, my brain its brain. It harvested my body, broke it down, and used what it could to augment itself. It's still my consciousness controlling it. But you won't see the man named Gabriel Roach again."

CHAPTER 52

No Choice

To meet Jake's charge, the alien mech had again gathered together a massive fist made from both of its hands—a writhing ball of steel waiting to cave in Jake's skull.

He channeled his rage into driving both bayonets straight through that fist. It shattered.

The mech shoved him away with the stumps where its hands had been, but right away, those hands began to reform.

Jake used his thrusters to counteract the trajectory his enemy had sent him on, and then he retracted his own hands, the segments of which were designed to settle around the extended bayonets.

Both rotary autocannons spun up, and he peppered the alien mech's face with armor-piercing rounds at point-blank range. It quickly became a pockmarked mess.

Even that began to reform, however, and the mech's arms were almost finished repairing.

Except, they didn't turn back into arms. Instead, they became twin energy cannons, which proceeded to pelt Jake with blasts of light.

Or at least, they tried to. Jake's focus was singular, honed by his anger, and he boosted left, resuming his steady rain of rounds, all down the mech's torso.

The mech turned to track Jake's path, and both cannons melded into one. An enormous buildup of energy began to take shape inside them, and Jake sensed that if that hit him, he would likely be vaporized.

He retracted the bayonets so that they wouldn't interfere as he wrenched his heavy machine gun from his back and fired round after round directly into the cannon.

The thing exploded with the energy backlash, the mech's hands once again becoming shattered stumps, though they quickly started to reform once more.

Not this time.

Jake engaged his thrusters at full power, hurtling toward the mech as it was busy healing itself. He extended both bayonets, and thrusting them forward, he impaled the alien mech straight through the center of its torso.

Even that didn't seem to slow it. It struggled against Jake's blades just as vigorously, using its truncated arms to beat at him.

With a titanic effort that made the dream flash scarlet more frenetically than it ever had, Jake pushed both bayonets apart from each other, widening the wound he'd made inside his enemy's chest cavity.

That done, he withdrew both blades, retracted them inside their sheaths, and let a grenade tumble out of one of his launchers. He seized the explosive from where it floated in space, and then he jammed it straight inside the alien mech's torso.

Rocketing away, he watched as his enemy pawed frantically at the gaping hole, trying to dislodge the grenade.

Unfortunately for it, its digits hadn't quite reformed yet.

As the grenade exploded, Jake helped it along by firing both his autocannons at full bore once again.

The flash was brief, but the damage dramatic—possibly irreparable. *So much for recovering this thing for study.* The mech was completely laid open, sheared almost in two by the blast.

Bronson appeared before him, his face scarlet, sweat dampening his forehead. "Good job. Now, I've lost almost two squads two these robotic killers. I can't afford for any more to get inside, Price."

"I'm on it," Jake growled. He grabbed his heavy machine gun from where he'd left it floating in space, and then he rocketed toward the destroyer, neutralizing robot after robot still swarming across the destroyer's hull.

After he took out his twelfth, the rest of the robots snapped their shield-like limbs downward against the ship, launching as one into space.

I guess they had enough.

"Sir, I did—"

"Not quite," Bronson said, appearing before him. "Behind you!"

Jake turned in time for the reformed alien mech to slam into him, driving him back toward the destroyer once more.

I can't believe it.

He managed to get his hand down to the EMP device clipped to the waist of his mech, and he activated it.

Both mechs crashed into the *Javelin*, becoming lodged in her ravaged metal hull. Paralyzed, Jake waited, pinned to the destroyer until Bronson sent someone to collect him.

It took the better part of a minute for Bronson to appear before him again, floating in space, wearing a strange expression.

"Price...how are you holding up?"

Jake stared at the captain, feeling as hollow as a mech without a pilot. The memory of the *Whale* disintegrating in an anticlimactic flash of light still stood out prominently in his mind. He expected it would for a long time.

Dad...

Jake had never truly appreciated Peter Price, and everything he'd done for him. He'd always assumed his father had been exaggerating, when it came to the horrors of war. The things you had to do, the things you had to witness.

Now, his father had proved his own point, in the harshest way possible.

"Where are those things headed?" Jake said, his voice devoid of emotion.

"Looks like they're on a course to intercept Eresos," Bronson said, and he clearly wasn't happy with about it. His tone carried a serious edge.

"Where did they come from? They looked like the same one my..." His voice hitched, and then he forced himself to say it: "The one my father dug up."

A third voice entered the conversation, then. "My theory is, after it escaped the comet where I found it, it must have gone to dig up its mates from other comets, to activate them."

It was Peter Price. He had appeared in front of Jake, alongside Bronson.

Jake looked from Peter to Bronson and back again. He shook his head to clear it, but his father remained.

"How...how are you here?" he asked.

"What are you talking about?" Peter said.

Then, Jake recognized Bronson's strange expression for what it was. Guilt.

"I did that," Bronson said. He hesitated, then spoke all in a rush: "I manipulated your lucid dream to simulate your father dying."

Peter stared at Bronson, looking aghast, and Jake did too, though the others couldn't see the expression he wore. If Bronson could have seen it, he would have felt very lucky that Jake was paralyzed from the EMP.

Because Jake felt like taking apart the man's warship, piece by piece.

"You monster," he managed at last, from inside his immobile mech. "You *bastard.*"

"I'm sorry, Jake," Bronson said. "I had no choice."

But Jake had no more words for the man. He waited for them to release him from his metal prison, and he mulled over what he would do next.

CHAPTER 53

Subsumed

Yes.

The way he bonded with the whispers, now...it reminded him of how he'd once bonded with his fellow Quatro. The way he'd shared in their fortune and misfortune, in their happiness and grief. All of the Quatro bound up together, as one drift, all progressing in the same direction.

Those days were past. Wound saw them for what they really were: an illusion.

And just look at the evidence.

The way even the Quatro in battle suits had fallen to the humans...that had been the universe administering justice to them, for their multifarious shortcomings.

There's only one Quatro I care for, anymore.

Wound did not even want to *consider* the four Quatro in battle suits who had fled and not returned. They were not worthy of having any thought devoted to them at all.

I do not care. Wound was digging toward the only Quatro he ever wanted to associate with again. They still had her inside the walls of Ingress; he was sure of it. The whispers had told him, and he believed everything those whispers said, because they would not lie to him. They *were* him.

The humans could seal off this tunnel if they wanted. Or, if they realized he was still here, they could come in to face him and he would kill them.

I will kill them all, for my mate. Even my own kind, if it comes to that.

Wound scraped a metal paw over the tunnel floor, wanting to spit. *They are my own kind no longer.*

He continued digging.

There was one who worried him...who he was not confident he could defeat. The human who had taken control of the bipedal mech that resembled Wound's own battle suit...the one who had led the four Quatro in battle suits away from the tunnel mouth...

That would be a fight Wound might not emerge from victorious, or at all.

Fear not that one, the whispers told him. *He will join us once we are through with him. A human subject merely needs more time.*

"More time..." Wound muttered.

More time. To join our drift. Our special drift. The true drift.

"Yes..."

The Quatro are used to considering themselves part of a larger whole, which is why you were...subsumed...so quickly.

"Yes!" Wound roared, then stopped, suddenly afraid those aboveground would hear him.

He continued digging. *No more distractions.* He'd keep working, keep digging, until he entered the city.

Nothing would stop him. He would be with his mate, then.

And together, they would slaughter everything that lived.

EPILOGUE

Progenitor

Bronson set his implant to "Do Not Disturb" mode and entered his office, making sure to lock the hatch behind him.

Only then did he permit himself to let loose the ragged sigh that had been waiting to come out ever since Jake Price had learned the truth of what Bronson had done.

The boy had taken it harder than even Bronson had expected. His people were in the shuttle bay now, extracting Price so that they could repair and reactivate his MIMAS. Bronson did not look forward to facing the boy, and he had no intention of being around him while he was piloting his mech. Not for a while, anyway. Bronson didn't actually think the boy would do anything to him, but he also wasn't an idiot.

A notification appeared in his implant's HUD—one that made his breath catch in his throat.

The Progenitors wanted to speak with him.

Well, he had a few things to say to them, in light of what had just happened.

He strode across his office, used his implant to open a panel concealed in the bulkhead, then slapped it with his palm. It registered his biometrics, causing the entire bulkhead to slide aside to reveal a robot that towered over Bronson by two feet.

He made it back to his desk chair before the thing activated, stepping out from its enclosure to tower over Bronson's desk. The machine was made of interwoven plates of silver- and gold-colored metal. It had no weapons, though Bronson felt sure there was power in those hands. Power enough to strangle him, probably, if it wanted.

You can tell by the way it moves.

But the robot wasn't here to strangle him. It was a telepresence robot, which the Progenitors used to interact with Bronson without actually having to be here. There was never any lag in their communications, as if the creature controlling the robot was somewhere on Bronson's ship, though he knew that was impossible.

As always, the Progenitor waited for Bronson to speak first.

"My sensor operator saw more of those little killers leaving other comets," he said. "All headed toward Eresos. What do you know about them?"

"They are ours," the Progenitor said. Its voice was baritone, though every word seemed to individually echo, or maybe stutter was the right word. Bronson wondered whether that was what the alien actually sounded like. Probably, the robot altered the controller's voice. For some reason, Bronson got the sense that it didn't want him to know anything about its actual appearance.

"*Yours?*" Bronson said. "They're under your control, then?"

"They are under the control of the directives with which we installed them. We left them behind, for the function you are about to witness them perform."

"They seem to be attacking Eresos," Bronson said, anger creeping into his voice.

"That is correct."

"What the hell, then!" Bronson yelled, jumping up from his seat, hands curled at his sides. "You assured me human settlements would only be threatened enough to drive contracts, not to endanger their very existence! The Quatro have already unwittingly created a boom for Darkstream. There's no need to send these robots!"

The Progenitor made its own fist, using it to lean on the desk and lower its head closer to Bronson's. "Have your profits not steadily risen? Has our arrangement not proved incredibly lucrative to you? Have you not built your entire society on the yield of our machines?"

"Well, yes..."

"Then you will continue to conduct wholesale surveillance of your population, and you will continue to give the data to us, wholly unfiltered. I advise you review the incredible dividends you are reaping as a direct result of our relationship, at such minimal cost to you."

Bronson's hands shook with impotent rage. "Do I have your assurance that human settlements will be left intact?"

"I assure you that our arrangement has not changed."

"Very well," Bronson spat.

Apparently finished with their conversation, the Progenitor returned to its alcove, which closed behind it.

Bronson sat back down at his desk, covering his face with his hands.

Acknowledgments

Thank you to Jeff Rudolph for offering insightful editorial input and helping to make this book as strong as it could be.

Thank you to Tom Edwards for creating such stunning cover art.

Thank you to my family - your support means everything.

Thank you to Cecily, my heart.

Thank you to the people who read my stories, write reviews, and help spread the word. I couldn't do this without you.

About the Author

Scott Bartlett was born 1987 in St. John's, Newfoundland, and he has been writing since he was fifteen. He has received various awards for his fiction, including the H. R. (Bill) Percy Prize, the Lawrence Jackson Writers' Award, and the Percy Janes First Novel Award.

In 2013, Scott placed 2nd in Grain Magazine's Canada-wide short story competition and in 2015 he was shortlisted for the Cuffer Prize. His novel *Taking Stock* was also a semi-finalist in the 2014 Best Kindle Book Awards.

Scott mostly writes science fiction nowadays, though he's dabbled in other genres.

Visit scottplots.com to learn about Scott's other books.

www.ingramcontent.com/pod-product-compliance
Lightning Source LLC
Chambersburg PA
CBHW061620190726
48288CB00007B/2402